TRUST

A WAVERLY BEACH MYSTERY

PAMELA M. KELLEY

TRUST
By Pamela M. Kelley

Published by Piping Plover Press
Copyright 2014, Piping Plover Press
All rights reserved.
ISBN: 978-1530710966

Edited by Bev Katz Rosenbaum & Judith Beatty
Cover Art Copyright by Renu Sharma
www.thedarkrayne.com

Please contact the author with any questions, at pamelamkelley@gmail.com

ACKNOWLEDGEMENTS

A special thank you to fellow writer and editor, Cindy Tahse Dickinson, for all of your support and editorial insight. You are a wonderful editor!

PROLOGUE

Twenty years earlier....

Melissa Hopkins wanted more than anything to be home in her warm bed, securely tucked under her thick down comforter. For several hours now, she'd been sitting in a small windowless room at the local police headquarters, being interrogated by the same two cops non-stop. It made her head ache, although she supposed the drinks she'd had earlier could be a contributor to that as well.

Most of her friends had started drinking a few years ago, around age fourteen. It was common in Waverly, a beach-front community that was busy in the summer and deadly deserted in the winter months. Her friends considered her a lightweight, as she had always said no, until a few months ago on her sixteenth birthday.

Melissa closed her eyes and tried to focus, and to remember what really happened, but her memory was a confused blur. She suspected she might have blacked out for a bit. That had happened once before when she'd been drinking vodka, and this time they had been playing quarters on the beach and doing shots. It was hard to play well on the sand, plus someone had the bright idea to mix vodka with orange juice and made the losers slug shots of the drink instead of beer. Melissa's stomach did an unhappy flip just thinking about it.

"Melissa, your Mom is waiting outside to take you home. As soon as you tell us what we need to hear, you'll be on your way. You want to go home Melissa, don't you?" The police officers seemed to taunt her. One was a tough looking Irish guy in his mid-thirties, who was clearly frustrated. The other cop was younger looking and equally irritated. They started in again, asking the questions they'd already asked, but this time she was hearing them differently. Her mind was too tired to protest.

"Melissa, the other two boys saw you run after Nancy with the murder weapon. Your prints are all over it, along with her blood. You were mad at Nancy—you admitted that already. You obviously did this, Melissa."

Melissa's head started to throb and she pressed a hand against her forehead, willing the pain to go away. "They saw me run after Nancy? Holding something?" It was so hard to focus. She had been mad at Nancy, furious even, but still, she wouldn't have killed her. She was sure of it. But it was all a bit hazy. She remembered running, falling and then waking up to a police officer shaking her and a flashlight in her face. She was still very confused and scared and was just sober enough to know that she was in serious trouble. Was there a chance that she could have done this? The police seemed to think so, and they said they had proof.

"Yes, Melissa. Just admit you killed her; all the evidence makes it very clear. If you confess, things will go much easier for you. You could be looking at much less jail time; a huge difference Melissa. We don't think you meant to do this. You didn't mean to kill her, right Melissa?"

"No, I didn't mean to kill her." Melissa felt bewildered, like she was being pulled underwater or in some kind of surreal dream.

"Say you killed her and you can go home. We can all go home." Their voices were kinder and softer now and Melissa really, really wanted to go home. She'd lost track of how many hours she'd been in this room, but it was much too long.

"I guess maybe I did it, I'm not really sure. I must have though, right?"

"Yes, good girl, Melissa. We'll go get your mother."

1

Lauren Stanhope stared out the window at the falling snow and marveled at the picture-perfect scene outside. It was just starting to get dark, and the dusky pink sky cast a warm glow over the neighborhood, which was a collection of meticulously maintained Victorian homes, many with intricate gingerbread woodwork now delicately frosted in a light covering of snow.

"You girls are so tiny," Nellie Chapman said as she pulled in the fabric around Lauren's waist tight and jabbed in a pin to mark the spot.

Lauren's friend and soon to be sister-in-law, Amy, snickered at that and Lauren shot her a look. Nellie was a sweetheart, and a close friend of the family, but she was also in her early 80's, and though she did fabulous work as a seamstress, she'd made the same comment at the bridesmaid fitting for Amy's wedding and took all their dresses in so much that they popped loose whenever they moved the wrong way. Though she'd agreed to use Nellie, Lauren wasn't going to let that happen again.

"Could you please leave it a little looser than you normally would? I have a tendency to gain weight when I'm stressed out. Better safe than sorry right?"

Nellie pushed her glasses back in place and glared at the spot she'd just pinned. With a painful sigh, she whipped out the pin and let some material out.

"I don't like it," she muttered as she jabbed the pin back in to its new spot.

"Thank you, that's perfect." Lauren smiled at the older woman who was still frowning at the beautiful wedding dress.

"Okay dear, leave it here in the dressing room. Amy and I will wait for you in the den."

Once Nellie and Amy left, Lauren peeled off the wedding dress and climbed back into her work clothes of gray flannel trousers and a soft caramel cashmere sweater. She peeked out the tiny window in the dressing room and got another little thrill from the sight of the falling snow. The first snowfall of the year always affected her that way; she got as excited as a little kid at the sight of the fat snowflakes drifting down. The cozy scene made her think of the warm feeling she always felt around the holidays and how she'd longed for years to create her own family and try to capture and keep that magical feeling all year.

Lauren still couldn't believe how much her life had changed in the past two years, moving back here, meeting David, falling in love and actually having that love returned.

She was tempted to pinch herself because it really did seem too good to be true that in a little over a month she'd be married and on her way to having the perfect life that she'd always dreamed of. She would hopefully even have a new home since she and David had been house hunting and found several houses that had potential. Still, she couldn't shake the feeling that it could all slip away in a moment, and that she was crazy to think she deserved to have that kind of happiness. She knew how quickly things could change when you least expected it. But, she reminded herself that it was just the nerves talking, and that it was normal for a bride-to-be to experience pre-wedding jitters.

"Lauren, your student is on TV, come quick," Amy called. She was one of the first people Lauren had met when she moved to town, as they were both teachers at the local high school. Lauren crossed the hall into a small sitting room, where Amy and Nellie were sitting on a cozy sofa and watching the news on a big screen TV.

"His name is Eric, right?" Amy asked, as the photo of the young teen flashed across the screen.

"Yes, Eric Armstrong. He's been out for the past three days. I thought he was sick. The flu has been going around something fierce."

"It's not the flu. He's missing. Do you think he might have run away?"

Lauren thought for a moment. "It's possible. I know he's been having some issues at home. We've met a few times after school recently, trying to figure out a way to help him focus better in class."

"Poor kid," Amy said.

"Let's hope he just ran away," Nellie said, voicing what they'd all been thinking. At least if he ran away there was a good chance he'd come back.

2

David Bishop had a standing dinner date every Tuesday night at Hannigan's pub. His grandfather was already seated at his usual booth when David arrived and joined him.

"Glad you could make it," was his grandfather's usual greeting, as if there was any doubt that David would be there. Both of them looked forward to these dinners. At ninety-one years of age, Gramps was all David had left for family and he really did enjoy his company. Gramps was still as sharp as a tack and had more energy than many people half his age. It had been difficult for David when he lost his mother to lung cancer just over two years ago, and his grandfather had been through a lot too, as he had also lost his wife. David's grandmother had passed away around that same time. David never failed to be inspired by him. Instead of shutting down, his grandfather had blossomed and turned into a social butterfly. Though the food was good at Hannigan's, his grandfather freely admitted that the people—particularly the young friendly waitresses who showered him with attention and laughed at his jokes—were the reason he came as often as he did.

"David, do you know Allison?" Gramps was chatting with a pretty blonde waitress who had just delivered his drink, a frothy Kahlua sombrero. Gramps wasn't a big drinker, but often had a single sombrero, which he said reminded him of a milkshake.

"Hi, Allison," David said as he sat down across from his grandfather.

"David's my grandson. He's getting married in a month." His grandfather beamed at that. He was a huge fan of Lauren.

David ordered a beer and they decided to split a pizza. They both agreed that the best thing on Hannigan's menu was the bar pizza. The rumor was that they'd bought the recipe from a restaurant in the next county. The crust was unusual, crisp and a little flaky. The tomato sauce was fresh and sweet and there was always plenty of cheese. Best of all, on Tuesday nights they ran a buy-one get-one special.

"This is the best deal in town," Gramps announced with enthusiasm as Allison set their steaming pizzas in front of them. As he always did, David agreed with him, and they dug in.

"Pity about that missing kid. It's been on the news all afternoon. You hear anything from Jake about it?" His grandfather asked as he reached for his third slice.

"No. I haven't talked to him in a few days. He's meeting me here a little later though for a drink. Have your guys heard anything?" Gramps had served as the town sheriff for many years and still kept in touch with some of the current officers who were sons of his former men. There was a small group of officers, most retired for many years, who met up every Saturday for lunch. Gramps probably knew almost as much as Jake did about what was going on in town, and Jake was the current assistant sheriff.

"Just sounds like he ran away. Shame, that. Kids feeling like they have to run away." Gramps finished off the last bite of pizza on his plate and dabbed at the side of his mouth with a napkin. "That was damn good, as usual."

"You should stay and have a drink with Jake. He should be here soon. He'd love to see you." David reached for the last slice; as usual, they'd easily finished one pizza and Gramps would take the leftovers home.

Gramps considered that for a moment. "Tell him I said hello. I can't stay though. I've had my one drink for the night; if I have another I'll be plastered."

David smiled at that. They both knew Gramps had never been 'plastered' a day in his life. One drink was all he ever wanted.

"Besides, Dancing with the Stars is on tonight. You know I never miss that. It's the results show." He was serious about that. Gramps was an excellent dancer and it was something he and his grandmother had always enjoyed, as she was a professional dancer when they first met.

After they paid the bill and his grandfather left, David moved to the bar to wait for Jake. The bar was getting packed now and he'd only just settled into his seat and taken his first sip of a newly poured beer, when someone bumped into the back of his chair, hard enough that he spilled a good half-inch of his beer.

In a second, Patrick, the bartender was there to mop up the mess. "Give me your mug," he demanded and David handed it over, watching with appreciation as Patrick topped it off and set it back down again. "There you are then, good as new." That was another reason they liked coming here. Hannigan's was a real Irish pub, the type of place where everyone really did know your name and if they didn't, it wouldn't be long before they did. They made you feel like a regular no matter how often you visited.

"Hey man, sorry about that," said a deep voice to his left. As it turned out, the man who'd spilled his beer was Randy Scribbs, a former fraternity brother that David hadn't seen in nearly fifteen years. Randy looked about the same. He was still a huge guy, well over 6' 2" and had dark curly hair that had thinned quite a bit over the years, not that David could say much there. He had grown to like the baseball cap look more and more for the same reason.

"Randy, what brings you to town? It's been a long time."

"My wife, Sharon, is pregnant and her family lives nearby, so we decided to buy a place here. I travel a lot for work and this way she'll have support close by."

"That's great," David said, glancing around the bar. Jake was running late as usual. He'd called earlier, said he had something important to tell him, and wanted to meet for an after work drink.

"So, I hear you got out of the baseball business?" Randy's

cheerful voice boomed above the crowd, and if you didn't know better, you'd think he was just a friendly guy. As if David had chosen to 'get out of the baseball business.' He'd been a rising star once, the scouts had all buzzed about his 'nasty stuff', the ultimate honor bestowed on pitching prospects. Until he blew out his arm in his third major-league start with the Boston Red Sox. A freak accident they called it and immediately shipped him off for the usual cure, Tommy-John surgery. But his arm was never the same and his career in baseball came to a quick end.

"Yeah, I got sick of it, too much travel." David took a long sip of beer and wished for a quick end to this reunion.

"Very funny. You were always a funny guy." Randy looked at him thoughtfully before adding, "I heard you're pretty good with numbers. Mark Tsongas said I should look you up."

David didn't see this coming at all. Mark was his biggest client and he wouldn't have guessed that he knew Randy.

"Yeah, I manage Mark's investment portfolio. We did okay last year."

"I heard it was way better than okay," Randy said with an enthusiasm that made David cringe. Where the hell was Jake? He glanced at his watch as Randy continued, "Mark golfs with Sharon's brother. I played with them last week and asked if they knew of a good broker. I sold one of my companies a few months ago and have a little money I need to invest. Do you have a card?"

"Sure, here you go." David dug into his wallet and then handed him a business card. When he looked up, he saw that

Jake had finally arrived and was looking around the packed bar. David waved him over and Jake squeezed into the seat next to him as Randy turned to leave.

"Gotta run. I'll call your office to set up a meeting. Great seeing you. Oh, hey, Mark also mentioned you're getting married in a few weeks. Hope this one works out better for you!" Randy slapped him on the back in farewell and then he was gone.

"Who was that asshole?" Jake asked as Patrick set his usual beer down in front of him.

"You really don't want to know. He's a former fraternity brother who just moved to town. The good news is, I probably have a new client. Bad news is, I have to deal with him."

Randy would have to remind him of Jillian. Even though it was over ten years ago, it still hurt to think of how she'd dumped him barely two weeks before their wedding because she 'just didn't love him enough.' You don't just bounce right back from something like that. He'd pretty much given up on the whole love and family thing until he met Lauren when she moved to town two years ago.

He'd always been skeptical of love at first sight, but he definitely felt it when his sister Amy, a ninth grade teacher, introduced him to her new colleague, Lauren. Lauren had lived in the area years ago into her early teens, and said she'd applied 'on a whim' when she'd seen the advertised opening. It was very different with Lauren. He knew she'd never pull the rug out from under him the way Jillian had. It was just easy with her because they got along great and trusted each other completely.

"David? Did you hear me?" Jake was looking at him expectantly. And he hadn't heard a word he'd said.

"Oh, sorry. I was just distracted for a minute. What did you say?"

"So you know that missing student? Eric Armstrong?"

"Yeah, I think he was one of Lauren's kids. Any word on him yet?" If there were any news, Jake would likely know of it.

"Nothing yet. The parents swear he'd never run away. That doesn't mean much though. Kids run away all the time." He paused for a minute, then added, "Did Lauren ever mention him at all? Say anything about him?"

"Are you asking as a friend or a police officer?" David teased. But the serious look on Jake's face told him he didn't think it was funny.

"Both, I guess. We're just digging everywhere we can, hoping to turn up something."

"Sorry. You know Lauren did mention that she'd been talking to him, trying to help him work through some things."

"What kind of things?"

"His grades had been slipping and it wasn't great at home. That's all I know. I'm not sure if Lauren knows much more than that."

"She didn't say anything else? Nothing else about the boy at all?"

"No, why? Has something turned up about him?"

"Nothing definitive. We've been going through his computer records and his online diary."

"Online diary? As in available to the public?"

"Yeah, connected to his Facebook page. Kids these days live their lives online—totally bizarre."

"Does he say anything that might give a clue as to if or why he ran away?"

"No. But he does talk about having a 'mad crush' on a much older woman. Someone he thinks about and sees every day."

David felt a sudden sinking in his stomach. "Do you have any idea who this 'older woman' is?"

"Nothing concrete, but we have to consider all possibilities and the strongest one we have so far is that it very well could be Lauren."

3

W ant to have a pizza at my place instead of going out?"
Lauren asked as they left Nellie's and headed toward
their cars. "The roads look like they are getting a little slick."
The original plan had been to grab a bite to eat somewhere
after the fitting. Amy and Lauren lived in the same condo
complex, so she could easily walk home instead of driving.

"Sure, I have a bottle of wine we can share too. I have a
case in the backseat—picked it up at lunch."

"A case?"

"You save a ton when you buy a case!" Amy said and
Lauren laughed. She knew Amy loved wine and had a great
collection. Lauren got her phone out and called in the pizza
order so they wouldn't have to wait too long.

They drove home and found the roads were slippery.
Lauren was glad they'd decided to just do pizza instead of
going to a restaurant. When they reached the condo complex

and parked, Amy followed her inside with a bottle of wine and started to open it. Amy had just poured each of them a glass when there was a knock on the door. Lauren wondered who could possibly be out in this weather. Maybe David was home and had his arms full. She opened the door and was shocked to find two policemen standing there.

"Lauren Stanhope?" the older of the two asked.

"Yes, that's me."

"Miss Stanhope, could we please come in? We'd like to ask a few questions." She let the officers in and invited them to sit at the dining room table.

"Can I get you something to drink?" she asked, and noticed the younger officer staring at the just opened bottle of wine. "Soda, water? Anything?" She added, so they didn't think she meant alcohol.

"No, thank you," the older officer replied and then added, "This shouldn't take too long." A moment later, there was another knock on the door and this time it was the pizza man. Amy jumped up to take care of it, and brought the pizza into the kitchen as Lauren went into the dining room to talk to the officers. She wondered if they were making the rounds and talking to all of Eric's teachers. She noticed that the two officers seemed a little uncomfortable, especially the younger one, who had pulled out a pad of paper and was staring down at it, doodling, while he waited for the older officer to start talking.

First, he introduced both of them. "I'm Officer Scott Gordon and this is Officer Chris O'Sullivan." Lauren smiled at that. Their names suited them. Scott looked to be in his early 50's, had closely-shaven gray hair, light blue eyes and a muscular build, Chris was likely in his mid-twenties, tall and lanky with an unfortunate shade of red hair. Like his partner, his hair was military short, his eyes blue, and his face full of freckles.

"We just have a few questions to ask you, about Eric Armstrong," Officer Gordon began.

Lauren nodded. "I'm happy to help. Do you have any leads yet?"

The two men exchanged a glance and then Scott replied, "Nothing of any substance yet, but we're working on it. So, tell me about Eric. I understand he was a student of yours?"

"That's correct. Eric was in my homeroom and also fifth period English."

"How did he do in class? Was he a good student?"

"At times. He was very bright and had a lot of potential, but he wasn't doing well consistently. I started meeting with him after class to see how we could help him focus better and to get him to open up."

"To open up? What do you mean?" Scott asked, as Chris looked up for a moment and then continued to scribble notes furiously.

Lauren tried to explain. "I immediately suggested counseling, that Eric talk to Betty Alves, our student psychologist, but he would have no part of it. He didn't know her and was afraid she'd call his parents."

"But he talked to you?"

"He didn't want to, not at first, but I told him that I was very concerned, and if he didn't open up to me I'd have no choice but to send him to Betty. He agreed to meet with me once a week, immediately after class every Monday for a month. We were just starting to make some headway when he went missing."

"What kind of 'headway' did you make?" Scott asked.

"Well, we talked about his study habits and ways he could focus better and be more prepared for class. He admitted that there'd been a lot of stress at home, his parents were not getting along and the constant bickering was getting to him. I suggested that he get out of the house to study, to go to the library and be a little more organized with his work."

"And it worked?"

"It seemed to. Once he removed himself from the stressful environment, he was better able to get his work done and was more engaged in class. I know he didn't like being at home, which is why I'm hoping he might have just run away."

"Right." Scott glanced at his partner and then asked. "Is there anything else that comes to mind? Anything personal that Eric may have told you? Did he have a girlfriend for instance?"

Lauren was surprised for a moment and realized that she had no idea if Eric had a girlfriend or not. "No. We never got into personal stuff. I don't know if Eric was dating anyone. I never noticed him with a girl."

"Okay, I think we're done here," Scott said as Chris closed his notebook. "We'll be in touch if we have any further questions. Enjoy your pizza."

The two officers left and Amy brought the pizza into the room, along with paper plates and napkins. She added a little wine to her own glass and saw that Lauren's was untouched.

"Drink up; I'm way ahead of you. I didn't want to be in the way so I stayed in the kitchen, listening and sipping. Pretty weird, huh? Them stopping by like this. Do you think they're going house to house?"

"I don't know. They were at school talking to some of the teachers earlier. I would have thought they'd just go back tomorrow to see the ones they didn't talk to today."

"Do you think he ran away?" Amy asked as she grabbed a slice of pizza and doused it with hot pepper flakes.

Lauren made a face at the sight of all that pepper. "I don't know how you can ruin a perfectly good piece of pizza."

"Don't knock it 'til you try it. It's delicious. Try a bite?"

"I'm all set." Lauren added a sprinkle of salt to her piece and then took a bite. She couldn't stop thinking about her missing student.

"I hate to say it, but I have a bad feeling about this. Things were starting to go better for Eric, his grades were improving, he was participating more in class. He was making progress. It doesn't make sense that he'd just take off."

"He's a teenager though. You said things were tough at home. Maybe something happened, a fight or something that set him off."

"Maybe. I hope they find him soon though. This is miserable weather to be out there alone."

"David is having a late night with Gramps." Amy commented as the clock struck 8:00 p.m.

"Jake was meeting him at Hannigan's for a drink."

"How is Jake? Is he still single? We need to find someone for him." Amy was always playing matchmaker. Not that Lauren could complain. She was good at it and said she'd known that Lauren and David would be great together.

"I don't think Jake has any trouble in that department.

David said women are always throwing themselves at him."
Jake was a handsome guy, with coal-black wavy hair and lots
of it, dark chocolate brown eyes and light skin, and at 6'4", he
was hard to miss. "Jake likes to date. I don't think he's anywhere near ready to settle down."

"He will be, when he meets the right one." Amy said with
certainty. "Not that I have any idea who that might be, but
you never know. I'll keep an eye out for him."

"I'm sure he'll appreciate that," Lauren said wryly.

An hour later, full of pizza and good wine, Amy pulled
on her boots, bundled up and headed out for the short walk
to her condo three doors down. Lauren was just about done
putting the leftover pizza in the refrigerator and the wine
glasses in the dishwasher when there was a light tap on the
door and then it opened and David walked in.

"Hey, honey," Lauren called out and as soon as David
shed his snowy coat, hat and gloves and stepped out of his
boots, she wrapped her arms around him and gave him a
kiss.

"Well, that's a nice welcome. It's miserable out there."

"How's Gramps?"

"He's good, same as always, flirting like mad with all the
young waitresses. He says hello."

"I had an interesting night," Lauren began as they headed
into the living room, and sank into the sofa. "Two police officers came here, asking me questions about Eric Armstrong,
my missing student."

"They came here? To talk to you?" David tapped his hand
against the coffee table and then said, "You know I saw Jake

tonight? Well he was asking me about you and Eric Armstrong too."

"He was? What did he say?"

"He wanted to know everything and anything that you've ever said about him. I could only remember bits and pieces. It's not like you talked about the kid all that much. I know you said he was one of your students that was having some trouble in class and at home."

"That's right. That's what I told the officers too. It's disturbing. I really hope he is all right." Lauren felt her eyes water thinking of her missing student. Where was he? Was he cold and scared somewhere? Was he ok?

"Jake said they found some stuff on Eric's computer and on his online blog. They think he had a crush on an older woman, maybe even had some kind of an affair." At the look of disbelief on Lauren's face, David added, "It happens. And here's the kicker, they don't know who this woman is, but they're wondering if it might be you."

"It's not!"

"Of course not. But, it is possible that he had a crush on you. I certainly wouldn't blame him." David grinned at that, but Lauren didn't feel like smiling. The very thought of what he was suggesting made her stomach turn.

"I suppose it's possible that he may have had a crush on me, but I really don't think so. I never got that kind of vibe at all. Not that I'd be looking for it though." She bit her lip, thinking back. Could she have missed the signs?

4

Lauren got into school a little earlier than usual the next day. Her habit was to stop at Starbucks along the way, pick up an extra-large dark roast coffee—she just couldn't bring herself to ask for a Venti. What was up with ordering in French? She never could figure that out. She liked to be in about an hour early, which gave her time to ease into her day and to get herself organized. She also enjoyed the peace and quiet, before the students rolled in and the day got under way.

The public school in Waverly was night-and-day different from where she'd been working for several years in an inner-city high school in New York, where gangs, drugs and single teen-age mothers were the norm rather than the exception. When Lauren first started there, she thought it was sweet that most of the students addressed her as 'Miss', assuming it was a sign of respect. Until one of the other teachers set her straight by telling her, "It's because they see us as interchangeable. We're all 'Miss', no first or last names. They don't want to really know us; they just want to get out." The thought depressed Lauren, especially when she found it was fairly accurate.

One of the things that had attracted her here was remembering how much she'd once enjoyed attending school in Waverly and how it still had such a quaint, small-town feeling. Waverly was an affluent seaside suburb of Boston. The town was large enough geographically that it felt spacious, and two-acre zoning in the majority of neighborhoods was a key factor there. The downtown Main Street area was still very much the same as when Lauren lived there as a child, with pretty cobblestone side streets and lots of little independently owned shops and restaurants. The waterfront area was her true love though. Lauren had always loved living near the water, watching the boats come in and out of the harbor and spending time at the beach. The best part about the condo she was renting now was that it was set high on a hill and had a panoramic water view. Although David was spending most nights at her place, he still had a condo as well. He owned a small flat just off Main Street that was an easy walk to his office.

Lauren couldn't wait to move into their new place. It was important to David that they had a house to move into once they were married, and they were cutting it close, but were scheduled to close a week before the wedding. They'd looked at a million places it seemed and Lauren was about to persuade David to sell his place and move into hers permanently, when something new came on the market, in a neighborhood that Lauren loved, but had long given up hope on. No one moved out of Waverly Point Beach, and even if they did, it was unlikely she and David could afford anything there. But the stars had aligned and the house that came on the market was perfect for them, and in their price range.

It was a small Cape, a recently renovated cottage that wasn't waterfront, but was near enough that they had some pretty views and it was only a short walk to the beach. They offered full asking price, as they knew they weren't likely to have a chance otherwise. Lauren sighed as she sipped her rich, fragrant coffee. Not for the first time, she felt as though her life was finally going exactly the way she'd always dreamed that it could. In less than a month, she'd be married and settling into her new house. She was really looking forward to it.

Bonnie Elliot, the school principal, poked her head in Lauren's office.

"Got a minute?"

"Sure, come on in." Bonnie stepped into the office and leaned against the door. She was holding an identical paper cup of coffee and took a sip before saying, "Are you up for golf on Saturday? I know you have a lot going on with the wedding coming up, but it's supposed to be unusually warm. There's no snow left on the ground and a few of us want to take advantage of it. What do you think?"

Lauren didn't hesitate. "I'm in. My clubs are still in my trunk. I almost took them out for the season last week, but now I'm glad I didn't." Golf was one of the things David had shared with her. She'd never played before meeting him, and now she was addicted. She and Amy played in a women's league at the local country club.

"Great, I'll set up a tee-time." She paused for a moment. "The media has started calling, asking all kinds of questions about Eric Armstrong. They're like wolves, chomping at the bit for any juicy morsel to run with. It's disgusting. I hope he comes home, or that the police find some kind of a lead soon."

Lauren murmured in agreement and gathered her materials up to head to class. Her joy at the idea of golfing on Saturday had faded at the mention of Eric and the reminder that he was also a golf fanatic and worked part-time at the country club, doing everything from gathering stray balls, to working the front desk, scheduling tee-times and greeting members as they arrived. From what she'd heard, he had a lot of potential as a real golfer too. *Come home Eric*, she pleaded silently. *Come home and get back on the golf course.*

5

For the most part, Jake liked living and working in Waverly. Like many of the guys here, his father had once also been a policeman in town and although Jake always wanted to follow in his footsteps, he didn't necessarily plan on doing it in Waverly. After college, Jake attended the police academy, joined the Boston Police Department and was thrown right into thick of things. He landed in Homicide, and after a few years, was promoted to detective. The work was thrilling at first and he felt like he was really making a difference. But as the years went by and the murder counts stayed steady year in and year out, it grew depressing. He needed a change, and at the age of thirty-five was thinking it might be time to settle somewhere. When he heard about the assistant sheriff opening in Waverly, it was a no-brainer.

He'd loved growing up in Waverly. The schools were good, people were friendly, his best friend David was living there again and the work offered a nice variety; not the volume of murders he was accustomed to, but he could live with that. In fact, it had been years since they'd seen a murder of any kind in Waverly. It was a quiet, safe town and he liked it that way.

He wasn't thrilled about the Eric Armstrong case though. Missing kids were tough. You hoped it was just a runaway situation, but those didn't always have happy endings. Sometimes kids were better off not returning home, yet life on the street was usually a worse alternative, but at least the kids were alive. Jake knew the unfortunate statistics too—that the longer a person stayed missing, the less likely they were to return or be found alive.

He didn't really think there was much to the older woman theory that was being floated around. Especially if they were pointing fingers at Lauren Stanhope. Sure, maybe he was biased because she was engaged to his best friend, but it just didn't add up to him. Still, they had to follow all leads, no matter how far-fetched they seemed. As he well knew after all those years in Boston, truth really was often much stranger than fiction and he'd lost track of how many times they'd said to each other, "You just can't make this shit up."

"Jake, we just got a call from a guy fishing out at Pine Pond. Says there's a dead body floating face down. You want to come with me to check it out?" Chris, one of the youngest officers on the force sounded excited and Jake couldn't really blame him. Dead bodies rarely turned up in Waverly. Jake wasn't nearly as enthused.

"Sure thing. Let's go."

6

David was not having a good day. He should be in a fantastic mood. He'd signed a huge new client earlier in the week, with the largest portfolio in the company's history. Who knew that Randy's 'little bit of money to invest' was actually a mountain of millions? He still didn't like the guy, and managing his money would mean talking to him on a regular basis.

His first taste of that was having lunch with Randy earlier in the day to go over the details of his investments. That part of the meal was interesting, but it wasn't where Randy wanted to focus the discussion. "I trust you to handle all the details, just send me good news in my statements and we'll be fine. Let's catch up on what we've been up to over the years."

Which meant Randy talked at great length about himself, his insanely profitable career as a motivational speaker, all the celebrities he met and lastly, much to David's disgust, he also shared a few too many details about the many women who regularly threw themselves at him. "They don't even care that I'm married. It's crazy."

After agreeing to 'do this again soon,' David had raced back to the office. He couldn't get away from Randy quick enough.

"Conference room. Now!" Billy Mosely, the firm's managing partner, made the announcement on the office loudspeaker. Billy and Chuck Evans were the co-founders of Brickstone Investments, the small, ten-person financial services firm that David joined over ten years ago. He'd gone to college with Billy, and when his baseball career imploded and he was hanging around Waverly, staying with his grandfather for a few months and feeling sorry for himself, he ran into Billy one afternoon at Hannigan's pub.

He was bored and trying to figure out what to do with his life and Billy suggested he work with them for a bit. They'd had a broker leave suddenly and needed someone to manage his clients. Everything was all set up, so it was mostly answering questions and sending updates to start. But it was a perfect transition, as Billy had suspected it might be. They'd both been economics majors in college, and David had always had an aptitude for numbers.

Everyone was in the conference room when David walked in and Billy handed him a glass of champagne. The mood was festive and David wondered what was going on. He'd been in such a funk all day that he must have forgotten there was something scheduled. Maybe it was someone's birthday. They usually broke out champagne and cake on birthdays.

"I'd like to announce, now that we're all here, that we are

making David a full partner, effective immediately! Congratulations."

"Cheers!" Around him, a sea of congratulations and clinking glasses swirled in his honor and David was truly dumbfounded and tickled. He'd thought a few times over the years that it would be great to be made a partner, but it never seemed to even be raised as a possibility. Billy and Chuck were the only two partners in the firm's history. They had started the company and he couldn't really blame them for wanting to keep it to themselves. After all, it still was a pretty small company.

He'd also briefly considered going out on his own a few times. Lauren had suggested it and he did give it some thought, but ultimately didn't think he was that much of an entrepreneur. He was comfortable here. He liked the people and he liked what he was doing. And then the light bulb went on. He'd just brought in a twenty million dollar account. Making him a partner ensured that the money stayed in-house, that David wouldn't leave to open up shop and take the firm's newest and biggest client with him. A client that size could keep a single firm afloat. He never would have left, but they didn't know that.

"This is certainly an unexpected honor. Thank you!"

He looked around the room and smiled. His day had turned around nicely, thanks to his new top client. So, why wasn't he more excited? Why did he have this nagging feeling that something was about to go very wrong?

7

Jake and Chris met the caller at the far side of Pine Pond, where it bordered the 16th hole at the Waverly Country Club. The fisherman was Norm Pollard, a retired mailman who had walked over from his house in Green Oaks, one of the country club developments. They almost didn't see him at first as his fishing spot was tucked away in the woods. But Norm was keeping an eye out for them and called out as they came his way.

"This is usually a nice, peaceful place." He said as they stared down at the body, which was nestled in a patch of lily pads and tall green plants that lined the edge of the pond.

Jake and Chris put their gloves on, pulled the body onto the grass and flipped it over. Chris took one look and then immediately stepped away and doubled over. He threw up until he was dry heaving. Jake could sympathize; he'd done the same thing when he'd seen his first dead body, which was also a floater—a mafia goon that they'd fished out of the Charles River in Boston. Dead bodies were disturbing enough, but floaters were among the most gruesome. After a few days in the water, a person is often unrecognizable due to rapid decomposition and other factors, such as being fish food.

Norm turned to Jake. "You think it's that missing boy."

"Could be." Jake wasn't sure, but thought it was likely. The size and approximate age looked about right. He lifted the body a little to reach the back jean pocket and removed his wallet. Everything looked to still be intact, several soggy dollar bills, a debit card, and a license.

"It's him." He called into the station to give the update and to make sure the regional forensics' team was on the way. They would have a lot to do at the site. Chris was back by his side in time to hear him give the news that they'd found Eric.

"Check out the back of his head. Looks like that's how he was killed. Wonder what they used? His head is bashed in good."

"The key question is who would do this, and why?" Jake said as he stared out at the water. "He wasn't killed here though; his body would have been discovered sooner. Norm, how often you fish here?"

"Couple times a week when the weather's good. I was here yesterday and a couple days before that—always the same spot."

"So he was likely dumped out in the middle of the pond and washed to shore."

"Which means we probably won't find a murder weapon," Chris stated.

"Hard to say. You wouldn't think so, but there's always mistakes made, and if we're on the ball, we'll catch it."

The forensics team arrived about thirty minutes later and got to work, marking the area and combing the surrounding areas for clues of any kind, like unusual footprints or anything that looked like it didn't belong. Once the area was fully investigated, the body was securely wrapped and packed into the van for transport to the coroner's office.

"All right, let's head back to the office now. Our work is just starting."

8

You're the calmest bride-to-be that I've ever seen," Amy commented as Lauren hung up the phone after confirming with the caterer that they definitely wanted to have a vegetarian option available. Amy had stopped by Lauren's office to chat about their days and walk out together.

"It's just that everything is all set. The only thing left to do is pick up the dress from Nellie's on Saturday. So there's nothing to stress about. Plus, it's still a few weeks away."

"I was a wreck. But it was mostly dealing with family squabbles—who was going to sit where, who wasn't talking to whom—that kind of thing. I lost ten pounds the week before the wedding."

"Well it's a good thing I'm not stressed out, because I'd probably gain ten pounds," Lauren said as she unwrapped a piece of chocolate and popped it in her mouth. "Want one?"

"I never say no to chocolate."

Lauren shut down her computer and stuck a stack of papers that needed grading into her purse. When she and Amy walked out of the office, they saw one of the officers that had stopped by her house the other night and a geeky looking young man with wild hair and a plastic pocket protector in his shirt walking down the hall.

When they reached her office, they paused and Officer Gordon spoke. "They found the body of Eric Armstrong a few hours ago. All we know so far is that he was murdered with some kind of a blunt instrument and his body dumped in Pine Pond. We have a warrant to check all of the teacher's computers, scan the hard drives, etc. It shouldn't take too long."

"That's awful!" Amy exclaimed.

"Horrible," Lauren agreed and unlocked the door to her office. "Help yourself, it's all yours."

Amy waited until they were outside before asking, "Why are they searching our computers? Do they seriously think one of the teachers had something to do with Eric's death? That's crazy."

"I don't know what they are thinking, and can't imagine what they think they're going to find. Jake told David that they found some stuff on Eric's computer that gave them the idea he might have had a crush or maybe even some kind of relationship with an older woman, possibly a teacher."

"Do they have any idea which teacher it could be?"

"I'm not sure how big their list is, but evidently I'm at the top," Lauren said with a nervous chuckle.

"You? That's ridiculous."

"It is, but David explained that they have to follow any

lead that comes in. Of course there's nothing to find, so they should figure that out pretty quickly."

"How annoying for you, though. Good thing you don't get stressed easily," Amy joked. "Having something like this happen to me right before my wedding would put me over the edge."

9

Jake and Chris pulled into the driveway of the Armstrong house, a modest, older ranch home that was in need of a fresh coat of paint. The lawn needed care as well; the grass was overgrown in some spots, patchy brown in others. Two cars in the driveway indicated that both parents were likely home. This was a part of the job that Jake dreaded. There was just no easy way to tell someone that a loved one had died. It was especially difficult when a child was involved. Children just weren't supposed to die before their parents did.

Chris stepped up and knocked on the front door, then backed down to let Jake take the lead and do the talking. The door opened and Judith Armstrong, a tired looking woman in her late forties took one look at the two of them and screamed for her husband Ted.

"Come in," she said with a catch in her voice. Ted stood behind her and put his hand on her shoulder. Jake sensed that they knew what was coming and were bracing themselves for bad news.

"You might want to sit down," he advised them and wordlessly they complied, sitting side by side on the living room sofa and waiting for him to continue.

"I'm sorry to tell you that we found Eric a little over an hour ago. His body was found out by the golf course at the edge of Pine Pond. We don't know what happened, but we're going to do everything in our power to find out. I am so very sorry for your loss."

"Why would someone kill my Eric? It just doesn't make any sense," Judith said softly as her eyes filled up and she looked at her husband with helpless confusion. He rubbed her back and didn't say anything. But then his voice choked as he thanked them for coming and asked what they could do to help."

"I know it's difficult to talk about this now, and I know you've both already talked to several of the detectives, but has anything else come to mind that you haven't mentioned previously? Was Eric seeing anyone or having any kind of relationship with anyone that we should know about?"

"The officers asked us the other day about this and I didn't think anything of it, nothing came to mind. I know Eric didn't have a steady girlfriend, but I've been thinking about this more and I don't know if it's relevant, but he did mention meeting someone after class a few times lately named Lauren. I just assumed it was someone he was in a class with, a study partner or something because he said his English grades were suddenly getting better. Like I said, I don't know if that's at all relevant. I just can't think of anything else."

"Thank you. We'll pass that along and dig into every bit of information we can come up with. If anything else comes to mind, please give us a call." Jake handed his card to both of them and then he and Chris left.

"That was rough," Chris said as they got back into the car.

"It never gets easier," Jake agreed as they drove the rest of the way back in silence.

10

Lauren walked into her house and as usual, immediately locked the door behind her. She felt compelled to check all the windows upstairs and down to make sure they were all locked and securely fastened. It gave her the chills to think that someone had murdered one of her students. As Jake had mentioned to them more than once, even though Waverly was a sleepy, safe town, bad things could still happen anywhere even here, so you had to always be on your guard and act smart. Simple precautions like locking all doors and windows were a must. True, if someone really wanted to get in, they could probably do it, but why make it easier for them? Jake had also told them that studies have repeatedly shown that, especially in a condo complex, thieves will always look for the homes with the easiest access, and an unlocked door was practically an invitation.

She'd stopped at the market on the way home and set about unloading her groceries and putting everything away, except for the items she needed to make dinner. David wasn't due home for at least another hour, which gave her plenty of time. She was going to make a wild mushroom and asparagus risotto with chicken from a store bought rotisserie chicken stirred in for some extra protein. If it were up to her, she'd have been satisfied with a vegetarian risotto, but if she'd served that David would have been looking around for the main course. He was a meat lover and if it was up to him they'd have beef every night.

Lauren set about to make the risotto. First, she finely minced a sweet onion and added it to the Le Crueset enamel-covered cast-iron soup pot that was already heating up a bit of olive oil. Lauren loved to cook; she found the whole process deeply satisfying and relaxing, especially something like a risotto, which involved constant motion—slicing, dicing, stirring, and tasting. Pure bliss. She smiled thinking of how David found it so difficult to comprehend that she truly enjoyed this. To him it seemed like so much work. His idea of cooking was slapping something on the grill and having dinner on the table ten minutes later. Quick and easy.

She measured out a cup and one-half of the Arborio rice, short round grains that would plump up when they cooked, and in a perfectly cooked risotto, would have just a slight chewy bite. She added the rice into the pan with the lightly browned onions and stirred until the grains were all lightly coated and shiny from the olive oil. A minute or so later she added a little white wine, and once that was absorbed began adding the main ingredient, chicken stock. She had another pan going on the stove full of rich, golden chicken broth, and added it to the pan a half-cup at a time, stirring and watching each addition until it was almost completely absorbed before adding more broth.

She'd also poured herself a small glass of chardonnay, even though she rarely had more than a few sips while she was cooking as she tended to forget the wine was there while she was in the zone of creating. Her mind often wandered as she stood over the stove, stirring and adjusting the heat every now and then so the risotto stayed cooking at a steady pace, which would ensure the right texture and chewiness. Even though she tried to focus on going through her mental checklist for the wedding, what she'd said to Amy was very true.

Just about everything was all set for the wedding, there were no last minute dramas yet that needed to be attended to. And so her mind kept drifting back to more disturbing thoughts, wondering what had happened to her poor troubled student and whether it was a random killing, which was almost too terrifying to consider as how can you really protect yourself against someone who just kills for pleasure? She knew that was rarely the case though, and that most murders were committed by someone who knew the victim.

She turned her full attention back to the risotto, which was simmering happily along, and added a mixture of assorted wild mushrooms and a pile of chopped asparagus. The risotto was at the halfway point and by the time it was done the vegetables would be cooked just the way she liked them and David would be home.

She took a sip of wine and then set to work on the chicken, slicing the meat off and using her fingers to pull it into bite-sized pieces, which she stirred into the risotto. She was just about to start the last step, when David walked through the door and the phone rang. She waved hello to David and grabbed the cordless phone in the kitchen. The number on the caller ID was one that she didn't recognize.

"Hello?"

"Is this Lauren Stanhope?" a strange female voice asked.

"Yes, who's this?" Great, a telemarketer, she figured. Why do they always call at dinnertime? She should have let it go to voicemail.

"This is Gloria Richardson from the Boston Times. Lauren, is it true you were having an affair with your student, Eric Armstrong?" Lauren was silent for a moment in shock. Before she could answer, Gloria continued, "Did you kill him Miss Stanhope?" Now Lauren was both rattled and furious. She'd been ready for a telemarketer, not this.

"No!" she said and slammed the phone down.

"That's the way to deal with a telemarketer." David came towards her with an amused gleam in his eye. "Forceful. I like it." He leaned in to give her a kiss and then sensed that something was wrong.

"Are you okay?"

"That wasn't a telemarketer," she said quietly and then turned back to the risotto, mechanically going through the final step of adding freshly grated parmesan cheese, butter and a small amount of broth. She turned off the heat, stirred everything together until it was rich and creamy and smelled amazing.

"Who was it?" David asked as the phone rang again, with another strange number on the caller ID.

"Don't answer it. Let it go to voicemail." Lauren quickly

checked the message that was left and as her churning stomach predicted, it was another news reporter. She filled David in on the first call and noticed his jaw clench. He was generally easy-going and that was the only sign that he was furious.

"First of all, it's ridiculous for them to make any kind of assumption—let alone accusation—and secondly, the kid was just found earlier today. How could you even be on the media's radar?"

"I don't know. None of this makes any sense." Lauren took a bite of the risotto, which was perfect, except that she now had little interest in eating it. Still, she filled two large bowls for the two of them and set them on her small dining room table, along with the parmesan cheese, as David usually liked to grate a little extra on top.

"Do you want some wine?" She asked. But David was already pulling a beer out of the refrigerator.

"No thanks, I'm good with this." They sat at the table and ate quietly. Lauren asked David about his day and her mood brightened some as he told her about the partnership promotion and his annoyingly lucrative new client.

"You'll meet him eventually and understand. He said he wants to have us over for dinner, raved about what a great cook his wife is. She's also eight months pregnant."

"I can't imagine she'd be up for entertaining."

"Yeah, he's a real piece of work. I'm sure that never crossed his mind."

"Well, we'll have to go out this weekend to celebrate. Maybe to that new steakhouse you've been wanting to try."

The phone rang again and they both tensed up. This time though, Lauren recognized the number.

"It's Jake." She said as she clicked to answer.

"Hi, Jake."

"Lauren, I just wanted to give you the heads up that the media has been calling us asking questions about you. I don't know how it got out that we were questioning you as we were questioning all the teachers, but somehow it did. You may get some calls from them as well, the vultures."

"Thanks, Jake. I already have, actually. It was a little surreal."

"No kidding. Well, it may get worse, just so you know. Until we turn up something else of substance, they don't have much else to run with. Tell Dave I said hello."

"Will do."

"Jake says hi," Lauren said when she sat back down at the table and picked up her fork. She was surprised to see that half her risotto was already gone and she'd barely tasted it.

"What did he want?"

"Just to warn me that the media might come calling. Apparently it's a slow news week."

11

So far, all the forensics reports had yielded nothing but inconclusive results. Jake stared at his computer and frowned. There was something they were missing.

"You really think that teacher might have done it?" Chris, the young redheaded rookie leaned against the side of Jake's desk as the other four officers gathered around. Every officer was on the case, and they were all in Jake's office sharing what little they knew and trying to come up with something that could move them forward.

"No. I know Lauren, and her fiancé is my best friend. There is just no way there was anything going on there, let alone a possible murder. We need someone else to focus on."

"So that's it, we're eliminating her as a suspect?" the older officer, Scott Gordon asked.

Jake sighed. "She's not a suspect, she's a person of interest, and no, we can't eliminate her yet. We have to follow all leads through, regardless of how we feel about them personally. Thing is though, she has no motive. None that I'm aware of. Anyone?"

"Well, she's getting married right? I heard the guy she's marrying just made partner at his investment firm; the guy's going to be set financially. Maybe there was something going on, she tried to end it and the kid freaked out, threatened to tell people," Chris said and then Scott added, "Sounds like motive to me. Not only would she lose the loaded fiancé, she'd probably lose her job too, as the kid was only fifteen and still a minor."

"Okay, I still say it's way off-base, but we'll see it through. Let's see what else we can dig up though. I don't want to get sidetracked on a wild-goose chase and miss catching the real killer. Chris, why don't you head back out to the golf course and see who you can talk to there about who they might have seen Eric talking to. He worked there after school and on weekends, right? Maybe someone noticed something, anything out of the ordinary."

"I'm on it," Chris said and stood up, ready to get going.

"Scott, why don't you visit the parents again. Try and get a list of every one of his friends that they know of and as much information on his daily routine. See what kind of changes, if any, there were within the family recently. Lauren mentioned that Eric had been having trouble studying due to problems at home."

"Bill, and Jim, why don't you guys head back out to the crime scene, take another look around, see if we might get real lucky and stumble onto a murder weapon." He grinned at that, knowing it was unlikely, as the area had been combed over thoroughly the day before, but it had been known to happen.

After the office was clear and quiet again, Jake continued to brood. He didn't like this case. Didn't like that people he cared for were being regarded with suspicion, and unless he was able to find a lead in a different direction, things were only likely to get messier for Lauren and David. The timing couldn't be worse given that their wedding was now less than three weeks away. For the first time, he missed the anonymity of being in a big city like Boston. It was easier to sleep at night when a potential suspect was a complete stranger. When the happiness and well-being of his friends didn't hinge on how well he did his job.

12

When Lauren arrived at school the next day she was dismayed to find several media vans waiting outside the front door. As soon as she approached the stone walkway towards the main door, they pounced. Cameramen and pretty young reporters flew out of their vans and ran up to her, all talking at once. "Lauren, can we have a word please? Lauren, can you tell us about your relationship with Eric Armstrong? Lauren did you kill him? Why, Lauren? Talk to us Lauren!"

The voices tangled together and morphed into a terrifying loud wave of white noise and Lauren felt claustrophobic. She couldn't get away from them fast enough. She kept her head down and ran to the front door. Thankfully, she realized that there must be some rule that they weren't allowed in the school, for as soon as she ducked in the door they fell back, disappointed but still hungry, like wolves all chasing the same elusive piece of meat.

When she got to her office, she peeked out the window to see if the vans were still there. They were. She'd never experienced anything like that in her life, and realized her hands were trembling and her heart was racing. She set her books down on her desk and turned on her computer. While it was booting up, Amy walked into the office.

"Are you okay? I heard those people outside were harassing you."

"Are they still out there?"

Amy pushed the curtain aside and stared out the window. "It looks like they're leaving. Bet they'll be back later, though."

"It's scary. I never could have imagined how it must feel to be mobbed by paparazzi like that. I can sympathize with celebrities that have to deal with it all the time. It's awful."

"It'll blow over. As soon as they find someone else to focus on."

"Let's hope that happens soon." Lauren shuddered and then changed the subject. "I hear they're making an announcement this morning, offering grief counseling for any students that are interested."

"That's a good idea. I hope they take advantage of it. It's got to shake the kids up when something like this happens, especially when it seems so random."

"I know. I ran around the house last night when I got home, making sure every window and door was locked tight," Lauren admitted.

"Good thing David's been staying over most nights. That must make you feel safer."

"Absolutely." Lauren knew she'd be a nervous wreck being

alone at night in the condo. She'd always been a light sleeper and whenever she was bothered about something, if she'd read a scary book or sometimes even watching the news, it could keep her up at night, jumping at every odd noise or the wind rattling against the window. Just knowing David was next to her ensured she'd get a good night's sleep. She couldn't wait to move into their new house. Just a few more weeks and they'd be married and settling in and hopefully, Eric's murderer would be behind bars.

All day Lauren kept getting hints of a strange vibe in the air. There was lots of whispering and muttering as she approached her fifth period English class, the one that Eric Armstrong had been in. As soon as she walked in, the room instantly hushed, and out of the corner of her eye she saw glances exchanged between some of the students. But then the class proceeded as usual and Lauren wondered if she'd just been imagining things.

After class though, when she entered the teacher's lounge she had a sense of déjà vu as the same thing happened. People stopped talking and looked away as she walked in, then a moment later they started talking again, but it felt overly animated and forced. Instead of lingering and making uncomfortable small talk, Lauren quickly got herself a hot chocolate and went back to her office.

Sure enough, when classes let out, Lauren saw the vans pull up out front again, waiting for her. There were more of them this time too. The numbers had doubled as word had quickly spread and everyone wanted to crack the story first.

"Maybe I should talk to them," she wondered out loud.

"What did you say?" Amy asked. She was waiting outside

the door as they almost always walked together and today Lauren was especially grateful for her company.

"Would it be better if I just state that there's no story here? That my relationship with Eric was nothing but appropriate—teacher and student—and that, of course, I didn't kill him?"

Amy pondered that for a moment. "I don't know. I think you should run that by Jake and David first and see what they think. There's a reason people say 'no comment' all the time. You know how the media likes to twist things."

"I suppose. It just feels a little like I'm trying to hide something if I won't even talk to them."

"I'd wait."

"Okay, let's go. We'll have to make a mad dash for it."

When they got to the front door, Lauren took a deep breath and then the two of them stepped outside. As soon as she was recognized, cameras started flashing and the reporters ran toward her, screaming out the same questions they'd asked earlier. But then, just as they were almost to their cars with the pack close on their heels, one of the voices broke through, "Lauren, by not talking to us you do realize you look guilty, like you have something to hide."

Lauren stopped in her tracks and turned around but still said nothing. The person who had spoken stepped forward. He was a male reporter, good looking with an air of arrogance about him. Sensing that he'd struck a nerve, he pressed forward, and asked in a singsong taunting tone, "Do you have something to hide Lauren?"

Lauren felt suddenly furious, and violated. Who were these people? She opened her mouth to speak and Amy tightened her grip on her arm, but Lauren pulled away and stared at the crowd, speaking to no one but addressing them all.

"Eric Armstrong was my student. Our relationship was professional and completely appropriate. I am saddened by this loss, but I assure you I had absolutely nothing to do with his death." She spun on her heels, waved goodbye to Amy, then unlocked her car and got in. She started the car immediately and drove off as quickly as she could. As soon as she turned the corner, she burst into tears.

13

He was killed by a golf club? No kidding?" Jake was on the phone with Phil in forensics.

"Yes, we were able to determine that it was likely a Titanium club, due to fragments embedded in the scalp."

"Amazing you could tell that it was a golf club let alone a Titanium one." Jake was always impressed by the detailed specifics that forensics was able to determine from a crime scene.

"It actually wasn't too difficult. A golf club leaves a very distinct impression in a skull."

"Great. Well, thanks Phil." Jake hung up the phone and called all the officers on duty into his office.

"So, we have something to work with now. Our boy was killed by a golf club. He worked at a golf course, that's a good place to start. Chris you went out there yesterday. Were you able to talk with anyone?"

"I talked to everyone who works there and a few of the

members that came through. No one remembers seeing anything out of the ordinary. Said Eric was a quiet kid, and a good worker. He came in, minded his business, did his job and left."

"Okay, well now at least we know what we're looking for. Let's head back out there and comb the entire area for that golf club. We need to search the entire perimeter of the pond as he probably wasn't killed in that area."

"What if whoever did this dumped the club in the water along with the body? Seems the most logical thing to do."

"Criminals don't always think logically. Especially when it comes to hiding murder weapons. That's where they tend to slip up. Let's hope that's the case here, because we don't have much else to work with. If we have to, we'll find a way to dredge the pond."

The officers filed out and Jake flipped open his notebook to review everything that they knew so far. Scott had talked with Eric's parents and got a list of all his friends. His parents confirmed that Eric wasn't dating anyone that they were aware of and they didn't know anything about his after school meetings with Lauren.

They weren't too happy to find out about it either, especially when they were told of Lauren's explanation that Eric was having trouble because of what was going on at home. Their immediate response was defensive and they denied that there was any truth to what she said. Essentially, they called Lauren a liar and that didn't sit well with Jake. He decided it might be a good idea to pay them a visit himself to clarify a few things—see what they had to say.

Jake got into his truck and headed out to the Armstrong's place, which was on the far side of town, a good twenty-minute drive. On the way out there, he passed the high school and saw the football team working hard at practice. Coach Burgess looked up as he sat waiting at a red light and waved.

As assistant sheriff, Jake was well known to many people in town, and even if they didn't know him, Waverly was still the kind of small town where people were friendly and would wave and say hello even to a stranger. He realized how much he liked living here.

He had a small, winterized cottage about a mile from the beach but high enough on a hill that he had a little view of it from his bedroom window. Only thing missing was someone to share it all with. He'd been thinking about that more lately, especially now that his best friend was about to get married and he had very few other single friends left.

He'd never thought much about it before, as he'd never lacked for dates. He'd never wanted to get serious with anyone before though, and now that he was actually considering the idea, he realized that he was in a major dry spell. He hadn't even had a date in several months. Problem with a small town like Waverly was that there weren't many single women he hadn't already dated. Oh well, it's not like he didn't have plenty of work to keep him busy.

He pulled into the driveway at the Armstrong's house and noticed that only one car was there. He wondered who was home. When he knocked on the door, Mrs. Armstrong lifted the shade first, peeked out the window and then opened the door.

"Hello, Jake. This is a surprise. Can I help you with something?" She had a pleasant and somewhat confused expression.

"I hope so. If you don't mind, I'd like to ask you a few more questions about Eric, make sure we're not missing anything."

"Of course, come in. Sit down. I was just reading here in the living room." She opened the door wide and he came in and sat in a chair adjacent to the sofa.

"Can I get you anything to drink? Coffee, soda, water?" Her voice quivered just a little and Jake felt for her. He couldn't begin to imagine how difficult this week must be for her.

"No, thank you, I'm good. I don't want to keep you long."

"That's quite all right. I'm happy to help." She settled on the sofa, and it looked like she'd been sitting there before Jake arrived, as a magazine lay open on the coffee table and a soft fleece throw was unfolded. She pulled the throw over her lap and waited for Jake to begin.

"I apologize if you've already answered most of these questions. I know this can't be easy for you, but we've found that often when we ask the same question a second or third time, we may get a slightly different answer, as you might think of something you didn't mention before."

"I understand."

"Okay, let's begin. First I want to talk about Eric's friends; who he was close with, if there was anyone he was dating?"

"I don't think he was dating anyone, at least no one that we ever saw or knew of. Eric was friendly with everyone, but he only had two really close friends, Peter Johnson and Ryan Mays. The three of them did everything together."

"Did they get along well? Had they been in any kind of a fight recently?"

"I really don't think so. They were all good kids."

"Were you aware that Eric was having some trouble at school? That his grades had slipped?"

"No, we didn't know. He'd always been a very good student. I had no idea that he was struggling in class. His last report card was excellent as usual." She hesitated for a moment before adding, "That was last year though, we haven't seen any of his grades yet this year, they don't come out for a few more weeks."

"And what about the reason why he was having trouble focusing? Eric mentioned to his teacher that there was some trouble at home and that you and Mr. Armstrong weren't getting along so well."

"There is some truth to that," she admitted with a nervous glance at the front door. Jake guessed that Mr. Armstrong was due home momentarily and probably wouldn't care much for the direction this conversation was going.

"The other day you and Mr. Armstrong were both pretty adamant that Lauren wasn't telling the truth, that Eric hadn't said anything about being unhappy at home. Why is that?"

"He can be difficult at times. He's been under a lot of stress, work has been slow and he had to lay two people off a few months ago. Guys that had been with him for years. He's been working extra hours to make sure all the work gets done. When he comes home, he's tired and short-tempered at times. I can usually read his moods, but not always quickly enough. He has a temper. If something sets him off he gets loud and sometimes a bit violent."

"Has he ever..." Jake began, but she interrupted him. "No, he's never touched either one of us. He just gets mad and smashes things. It doesn't last long though. I never realized how much it must have bothered Eric. He never said anything," she said softly and her eyes were wet.

Jake decided it was time to change the subject, get back to an easier question.

"When was the last time you saw Eric? When did he disappear?"

"Five days ago on Saturday afternoon. He was heading out to work the morning shift at the country club. He never came home. I don't think he ever made it to work either."

The club manager had confirmed that Eric didn't show for work that day. Which meant he'd likely been killed in the early morning hours when it was still dark out.

"Where were you and Mr. Armstrong that day?"

"We were both home. Ted was working out back in his shed. He does woodworking as a hobby, mostly wooden boat models. He loves working on boats of all sizes."

"Does he own a boat?"

"He keeps a small dinghy down at the pond. Ted also loves to fish. He'll disappear for hours sometimes, just sitting out there in his boat waiting for a fish to come by."

At that, the front door opened and Ted walked in. He looked surprised and not overjoyed to see Jake engaged in conversation with his wife.

"What's going on?" he asked gruffly as he shook off his coat and stepped out of his work boots.

"Hi honey. Jake was just asking a few more questions."

"What's left to ask? Didn't we cover everything the other day?"

"We just don't want to miss anything. We're determined to find who did this to your son, Mr. Armstrong."

"Good. We just about done then?"

"Just about. Oh, do you golf, Mr. Armstrong?"

"Used to. Not so much anymore, too busy. Why is that important?"

"Just wondering how Eric became interested in it. I heard he was pretty good."

Ted puffed his chest out a bit at that and his voice sounded a little friendlier. "Taught him myself when he turned five. We used to spend a lot of time together on the course." Jake decided to end the conversation on a high note.

"Well, I think we're good for now. Thank you both for your time." He stood up and turned toward the door. Judith jumped up to open it for him.

"We're glad to help and appreciate everything that you're doing. Don't hesitate to call again if you need anything else."

"I'll be sure to do that. Good night."

Jake walked back to his car and glanced back at the house. The shed door was ajar and he could see what looked like half of a small wooden boat on a workbench. He wondered what his real boat looked like. Neither of the Armstrong's was considered a suspect, although their only alibis were each other. Technically, they still needed to be officially ruled out. He'd have to go get a look at that boat on Pine Pond for starters.

14

Lauren almost ran a red light on her way home. She just couldn't get there fast enough. She was sill sniffling as she pulled into her parking spot and ran into the house. She threw her stuff down on the kitchen table and went upstairs to draw a bath, and added a generous amount of bubble bath to the water as it poured in. One of her favorite ways to unwind after a stressful day or when she was really upset about something was to sink into a relaxing, hot bath.

She undressed and dipped a toe in the water. It was just hot enough and she stepped in and sat back with her head leaning against the side of the tub. She tried to empty her mind and just let the warm water wash over her. It felt wonderful and she lost track of how long she had laid there. She didn't want to get out of the tub—it was so nice to just float and think of absolutely nothing. But eventually, the water started to cool and the troublesome thoughts began to creep back in.

How bad was this going to get? She knew from personal experience that it didn't always matter so much whether someone was guilty or not. Once word got out that she was even considered a 'person of interest', there would be many who would consider her guilty as charged. Where there's smoke, there's fire, you know. Since the media vans were there today, she knew that her life was about to change.

She'd be on the news tonight and in the papers tomorrow morning. It didn't matter that she wasn't an official suspect, or that they had no real suspect or any evidence to tie her to anything. It was becoming public knowledge that she was being looked at, and that alone would be damning. She wondered what it would mean for her job. There were bound to be parent protests, and in a way, she couldn't blame them. If she were in their shoes, she'd be concerned too.

Reluctantly, Lauren eased out of the tub and wrapped herself in a thick soft towel. Half an hour later, with shiny dry hair and in her favorite velour sweats and a big fisherman knit sweater, she padded downstairs and poured herself a small glass of chardonnay. David had called earlier and said he'd bring home some Thai takeout. She figured she had about an hour before he arrived and could probably get through grading most of the stack of papers she'd brought home.

Almost exactly an hour later, she finished grading her last paper and put the stack back in her bag to bring in to work the next day. It was a few minutes before six, so she clicked on the TV, dreading the evening news, but knowing she needed to know what she'd be dealing with tomorrow.

David came in the door just as the news started. Lauren got a couple of paper plates and they settled on the living room sofa with the takeout cartons lined up on the coffee table. They dug in as the broadcast started, and sure enough, it didn't take long for the coverage to begin. In fact, Lauren was the lead story for the night.

Mary Piper, a perky, twenty-something brunette with a gleaming smile and perfectly styled hair started things off: "Tonight we're bringing you the latest on the shocking disappearance and murder of a young Waverly teen. His teacher, Lauren Stanhope is officially a 'person of interest' as there seems to be some question as to whether or not the two were having a romantic relationship. They were admittedly meeting secretly after class and Eric's grades took a sudden upturn in the past few weeks. We spoke with the teacher, Lauren Stanhope, earlier today and have live coverage of her statement after the break."

"You spoke to them?" David put down his fork and looked at Lauren in surprise. "Why would you do that?"

"I felt like I had to. If I hadn't said anything, they would have shown coverage of me running away from them, looking guilty. This way I stood up for myself. I was pretty upset."

After the break, they aired the video of Lauren. She cringed at the crazed hunted expression on her face and wondered if she'd done the right thing. Maybe she should have kept quiet, said nothing and waited for it to all blow over.

"I didn't realize how bad they were," David said as the segment ended and the weather forecast began. "I think you did the right thing. They would have worn you down eventually. Better to come out fighting, I think."

PAMELA M. KELLEY

"I don't know," Lauren said doubtfully. "I looked a little unhinged."

"You looked upset and who wouldn't be? I don't understand how they can air stuff like this, to put it out there that you are a suspect when they have no evidence of anything. It seems wrong."

"But I'm not a suspect, I'm a 'person of interest', which is significantly different, yet I doubt most people watching the broadcast will realize that. They'll just assume I'm guilty of something."

They finished eating in silence and when done, David leaned back and said, "Let's go away this weekend, get out of town and just relax. Maybe go to that bed and breakfast up in Maine you've mentioned before. We can eat lobster, have blueberry pancakes for breakfast, and forget about all this insanity for a few days.

"That sounds heavenly. First, I have to get through tomorrow. Thank goodness tomorrow is Friday." Lauren also knew she was going to have to share something with David that was a chapter she'd long ago shut the door on. More than once, she had considered telling him about what had happened nearly twenty years ago, but that was something from her past that wasn't relevant now and things were so good between them. Lauren just wanted to forget that awful night and the aftermath that followed.

15

L auren expected that the media vans might be at the school again; what she didn't anticipate was that they'd be parked right outside her condo, waiting to pounce the minute she walked outside.

This time she chose to ignore them. There was nothing further she had to say and she sensed that anything she said wasn't likely to help her and would just give them more of an opportunity to make her look horrible on air. So, she kept her head down, refusing to give them any kind of a camera shot and hurriedly made her way to her Honda Civic, then sat there steaming, waiting for one of the vans to move since she was completely blocked in. While she was waiting, the cameramen and reporters swarmed around her car, knocking on the window to get her attention, trying to get her to look their way, but instead, she put her sunglasses on and looked straight ahead. As soon as the van moved out of the way, she pulled out.

There was only one van parked outside the school, so she was able to avoid them easily, hurried right inside and went to the cafeteria to get a coffee. She'd been so rattled and eager to get away from the media that she'd forgotten to stop for her usual Starbuck's fix. Once she had her coffee, she headed to her office and found Amy waiting there for her. She handed Lauren copies of both the local and Boston papers. Lauren glanced at the covers and then immediately felt faint. She grabbed onto the side of the desk and then sat in her chair.

"Are you all right? You look as white as a ghost."

"I'm ok. I knew there'd be coverage today, but I didn't expect that." They both looked at the front covers where Lauren's picture was front and center, and her name in giant bold letters. The local paper wasn't as sensationalistic as the Boston one, which had more of a tabloid look to it. The headline made both of them cringe, "Forbidden love affair gone bad?" and below that in just slightly smaller letters, "Did this single teacher turn to murder to cover up her relationship with an underage student?"

"Why do I feel like I've done something wrong?" Lauren was dreading facing her first class. "I'll have to say something to the students, reassure them this is nothing but speculation and that there's no truth to it."

"Let's discuss that. If you could, please come by my office for a moment, Lauren." Emily Morehouse, school principal was standing in the doorway.

"I'll catch up with you later," Amy said as Lauren got up to go to the principal's office.

Lauren had always admired Emily Morehouse. She was a warm, smart and funny woman who had been principal for over ten years. The teachers loved her and the students respected her. Emily walked back to her office and Lauren joined her a few minutes later.

"Please, have a seat," Emily said as she shut the door firmly behind them and then sat down at her desk, facing Lauren.

"We need to handle this carefully." She began. "As you can imagine, I've had a number of calls already from concerned parents. I've reminded them that you have not been charged with any kind of a crime—that you are just being questioned along with many others as the police seek to find whoever did this."

"Emily, I can assure you that there's nothing to this..."Emily put her hand up.

"I know. I've talked with Betty, and she filled me in on how the two of you had discussed Eric and that he was hesitant to meet with her, afraid that it would get back to his parents. I also know that his talking to you obviously was helping. His grades were showing marked improvement."

"He was having trouble focusing at home. I suggested he get out of the house more, go to the library or to a friend's to study."

"I think, instead of you speaking with each class, I will make an announcement during home room, letting the students know that you have our complete support and that they should disregard the rumors swirling in the media. Let me know if you run into any problems."

"Thank you. I will. I really appreciate your support, it means a lot to me."

"You're important to us, Lauren. I've always been a firm believer in dealing with facts, not speculation."

The rest of the day passed in a somewhat uncomfortable blur. Lauren sensed the confusion emanating from her students. Despite the principal's announcement, many were unsure and curious if there was anything to the rumors. She overheard bits and pieces of conversation as she passed through the halls.

"I heard the wedding's off, that her fiancé caught them together."

"I thought Eric was gay, who knew?"

"Miss Stanhope is as straight as an arrow, no way there's anything to this."

"Man, how did Eric do it? She's hot!"

When the last bell rang, signaling the end of school for the day, Lauren wrapped things up quickly and then stopped by Amy's office.

"I'm glad that's over." She said.

"You're all set to go already? I still have a few things to finish up."

"No problem, I'll catch up with you on Monday. David's taking me away for the weekend. I am really looking forward to it." She told Amy about the Bed and Breakfast in Maine.

"That sounds heavenly. Mark and I went up there about six months ago. You're going to love it. Don't even think about the madness down here. It'll do you good."

"That's what I'm counting on."

16

David was having the longest golf game of his life. Randy had called earlier in the week and suggested they get together Friday afternoon for a round of golf at the club. He tried to demur, saying he was going away for the weekend and had too much to get done before he left. But then Randy threw out his trump card. "Billy and Chuck are in and they said they're looking forward to it and to tell you they'll be expecting you to be there."

So for over two hours now they'd been listening to the Randy show—non-stop chatter about his many successes and plans for the future. Billy and Chuck seemed genuinely interested, impressed even, but David kept checking his watch. He was eager to finish up and get on the road with Lauren. He was glad that no one had mentioned anything about her or the Eric Armstrong murder. It was the last thing he felt like talking about, especially with Randy and his partners.

"So, David, where did you say you and Lauren are off to this weekend?" Billy asked as they approached the 18th hole.

"Kennebunkport, Maine. There's a bed and breakfast Lauren has been dying to go to."

"How is Lauren doing? Holding up okay?" Chuck asked.

"She's good, looking forward to a weekend away though."

"How long have you two been dating?" Randy had a curious look on his face.

"Just about two years now."

"That's not a very long time though, is it? I mean to really know everything about a person?"

"What are you getting at?" David felt his jaw clench.

"Nothing, not a thing at all. Just thinking out loud. I've been married for ten years now and still keep learning things about my wife; things I never would have guessed years ago. She went through a shoplifting phase when she was in high school. All her friends were doing it, but she was the one who got caught. Ended up doing community service or something so it wouldn't go on her record. I'm just saying—there might be things you don't know about her."

"Lauren's a great girl," Billy interjected as he saw the anger flash in David's eyes and shot him a look warning him to stay calm.

"I think I know everything I need to know about Lauren," David said quietly.

"Hey, I'm sure you do. You have a good weekend now." Randy turned to the other two men, "All right then. Great game. Who's ready for a cocktail? David...one for the road?"

"I'd love to," he lied. "But I have to get going since Lauren wants to try and get up north before dark."

17

The ride up to Kennebunkport was a relaxing one. David drove and they left early enough that they managed to miss the rush hour crush. By an unspoken agreement, they didn't talk about the Eric Armstrong case once. They listened to all their favorite CD's—Pearl Jam, the Stones, Billy Joel and Elton John, and Lauren's newest discovery The Fray. It was just getting dark as they entered Kennebunkport and found their bed and breakfast, The Road's End.

Amy had raved about this place when she and Mark came here back in the spring for their anniversary. As they stepped inside, and walked toward the front desk, Lauren felt a wave of peace wash over her. The atmosphere was wonderful and calming. There were thick scented candles placed around the lobby area and she picked up a hint of vanilla or a freshly baked cake. The inn was lovely and beautifully decorated with delicate patterned wallpaper in soothing colors of soft blue and sea foam green, accented with cream painted wood. An older woman with a preppy salt-and-pepper bob and fashionable reading glasses, sat at the front desk and smiled as they walked in.

"Welcome to The Road's End. I'm Ethel Murphy. May I help you?" She asked in a distinctive Maine twang.

"We have a reservation, under David Landers."

"Of course. Yes, here we are. Oh, and you're in luck. We had a cancellation for this weekend for our honeymoon suite, so we put you in there. I thought it was appropriate as Mr. Landers mentioned that you're due to be married in a few weeks."

"That's wonderful," Lauren exclaimed. And it was. Ethel showed them to the suite which was on the second floor, overlooking downtown and the harbor. There was a gas fireplace, which cast a warm rosy glow over the already cozy room. The bed was a queen-sized sleigh bed of dark wood, topped with a pile of plump pillows and fluffy down comforter with a matching coverlet all in soft elegant shades of cream. There was a sitting room with a small sofa and table, and the bathroom was amazing. It was huge, with a Jacuzzi and a large glass door shower.

"We serve a hot breakfast from 7:00-10:00 a.m. Come down anytime during those hours. And if you need anything, at any time, call the front desk. Someone is always there. Oh, and there's a mini-refrigerator over there." Ethel pointed to a small cubby just below the main bay window and padded window seat. "There's a complementary bottle of champagne to welcome you. Enjoy your stay!"

She left the room, closing the door gently behind her.

David and Lauren looked at each other and smiled. "This was such a good idea," Lauren said as she took the bottle of champagne out of the mini-fridge, opened it and poured two glasses.

David lifted his glass and tapped it against Lauren's in a toast, "To a great weekend, and to our future together."

"And to everything going smoothly at the wedding. I can't believe it's just a few weeks away." It seemed so close and yet so far.

The weekend flew by. They dined on baked stuffed lobster in the evening and enjoyed blueberry pancakes and plump sugar-topped muffins bursting with fresh blueberries at the morning breakfasts, served in the formal dining room downstairs.

Everything was perfect until the ride home. Lauren was driving this time and David's mind kept drifting back to what the ever-annoying Randy had said. He totally trusted Lauren, but was curious to know more about her. She never had shared much about her past before moving back to Waverly; only that her parents had died in a car crash years ago and that she'd been raised by her Aunt who lived in Connecticut. She was an only child as well, so didn't have much in the way of family. Unlike David, who'd grown up in a large extended family with lots of cousins, aunts and uncles. The holidays were like crazy sprawling reunions, complete with a kids' table and adults' table with people running around and food everywhere. His family was Italian, and every gathering revolved around food—an abundance of it.

"So, do you have any deep dark secrets you haven't told me?" he said in a teasing tone.

"What?" Lauren had been lost in one of her favorite Pearl Jam songs, the slow rhythmic Wish List. David's question jolted her out of her happy music trance.

"When we were golfing with Randy the other day, he was just saying how he's been married over ten years and still keeps discovering things he never knew about his wife. Like that she went through a shoplifting phase when she was a teen."

"I never shoplifted," Lauren said as she shifted lanes to pass the car in front of them.

"No, I never pictured you as a shoplifter. So, you have no skeletons in your closet? No ugly surprises you might spring on me one day?" he asked with a smile.

Lauren glanced over at him and opened her mouth as if she were about to speak and then just shook her head and turned her attention back to the road.

"What? Is there something? What were you about to say?"

"Well, I never really *did* anything, but I did once *confess* to doing something. Three of us did, but it was thrown out by the courts."

"What do you mean? Why would you confess to something you didn't do? What did you confess to?"

"Murder."

18

❧

"You're kidding, right?" David couldn't imagine that she was serious.

"No, I'm not kidding, unfortunately."

"What happened? And why did you never mention this before?"

Lauren bit her lip for a moment. "Two reasons. First, it's something I don't talk about, having been a long time ago and I prefer not to go back there. Second, I was innocent and the confession thrown out, so there were never any charges. So, it's like it never happened."

David thought about that for a bit. "But it did. And you still haven't told me exactly what happened, why you would confess to something you didn't do?"

"To be honest, it's all a little hazy. It was the same way back then too—it was always a blur. I was sixteen, and a bunch of us were playing miniature golf at that old course by

the beach—you know the one off Silver road?" He nodded
and she continued. "Well, it was late on a cloudy Saturday
afternoon and the miniature golf place was getting ready to
close up early as business was slow and the sky was dark,
threatening rain. Someone suggested moving the party up
the road to the beach where someone's brother had a cottage
and would buy beer for us."

"You were drinking beer at sixteen?" David was surprised.

Lauren chuckled nervously. "Most of them started a year
or two earlier, actually. We'd drink on the beach. It was stupid, but we were bored and curious."

"How many of you were there?"

"About ten I think. Half girls and half boys. There were
only a few couples but it was mostly just friends and some
innocent flirting."

"So, you were drinking at the beach, then what happened?"

"It got dark and late and we all sort of lost track of time a
bit. We'd been playing drinking games and most of us had too
much. We didn't handle liquor so well back then and didn't
know how to judge when we'd had too much."

"This is really surprising to me, considering you rarely
have more than a second glass of wine now."

"I never loved the drinking, not like some of the others
did. What happened that night stayed with me. I just went
along with the crowd to be social. Things got a little ugly
though, as a few of the guys started fighting. They were both
interested in the same girl, Nancy Hines. It was stupid. She
got upset and ran off crying, and after a while, everyone kind

of scattered and drifted home. I went to leave when most of the others did, a few of the guys stayed behind to go after Nancy and calm her down."

"So who was murdered?"

"Nancy. The police found her body two hours later behind a dune. Someone had called them on us because we were being loud. They just happened to find her as they were walking around yelling at us. They hauled all of us in for questioning. After a while, they let the others go, but they kept me and two of the boys behind."

"But if you left before the others did, why would they focus on you?"

"I had dated one of the boys; we'd only gone out a few times, but I was crazy about him, and devastated when Nancy Hines started flirting with him and he dropped me to go out with her. A few of the other kids had told the cops that and they said it gave me motive. I was pretty jealous and upset, that's for sure, but not enough to kill someone!"

"So, why confess then? How does that possibly happen?"

"It used to be quite common actually. All three of us confessed and they were later deemed false confessions. We were coerced."

"All three of you? That's so bizarre. How did they do it?"

"We were just kids and they basically scared us into confessing. I'd told them I'd been drinking and was confused about what happened when, and couldn't remember everything. I think I actually may have blacked out for a period and they hammered me about that. Kept saying if I couldn't remember, how did I know for sure that I hadn't done anything? They reminded me of how angry I was at Nancy and they almost made it sound reasonable. I actually started wondering if maybe I had done something. They kept us there for hours, asking us the same questions over and over again. And they lied. They told me that the other two boys said they'd seen me chase after Nancy carrying something in my hand and then I disappeared. They didn't see me again that night, so I must have done it. They made me doubt myself. And they didn't give us anything to eat or drink for hours. I had to beg to use the bathroom. It was awful."

"They did the same to the others?"

"Yes, they had us in separate rooms and they told all kinds of stories, making us think the other two had seen something that proved the other person was guilty. Finally, I was so exhausted and confused that I actually started believing I must have done it. So, I sort of confessed. At that point I wanted to go home more than anything else."

"So, how did they rule that it was a false confession?" David was fascinated by what Lauren had told him and a little disturbed. It was a side of her that he'd never been granted access to before.

"One of the boy's fathers was a defense attorney. He demanded access to the interrogation videotapes and filed a petition to have the confessions dismissed, as it was clear that all three were coerced."

"Did they ever find the real killer?"

"No, they never did."

"How was she killed? What was the murder weapon?"

"A miniature golf club. One of the kids had grabbed one and brought it with us to the beach."

"Really? Couldn't they tell who did it by the fingerprints?"

"No, because all of our fingerprints were on it. We made up a drinking game using the club and a few extra balls that someone had. Everyone took a turn swinging that club. So, the results came back as inconclusive."

"Well, that's quite a story." David reached his hand over and touched Lauren's briefly. "Thank you for telling me."

"There's something else." Lauren began cautiously.

"What?"

"We moved away after that summer. Even though our confessions were tossed out, and the media wasn't as bad in those days as it is now, it was still pretty bad. Our case was somewhat groundbreaking then and there was a lot of coverage because of the false confession aspect. There had been another similar case where three boys confessed to a murder none of them committed and their confessions also thrown out, and the murderer—an older man—caught soon after. These cases resulted in the law, changing how interrogations were conducted, really clamping down to stop the abuse, especially as it could result in a wrongful arrest and verdict, and worst of all, that the real murderer gets away with it."

"I didn't realize that."

"We moved far away, clear across the country to Seattle. My parents had divorced during the summer and my Mom decided to take back her maiden name, Stanhope. She suggested that I do the same, and she also thought it would be a good idea to start using my middle name, so it would be a completely fresh start, so we legally changed it."

"I thought your middle name is Melissa?"

"It used to be Lauren."

19

On his way home from work the next day, David swung by his grandfather's house. It was only Monday and they'd be seeing each other the next night for dinner, but still David had a strong urge to go talk to him. He was easy to talk to and sharp. He'd always enjoyed bouncing tough problems off him. He'd called first to tell him he was going to come by, but there was no answer. With most people, he'd assume that no one was home, but with his grandfather, he knew he had a good fifty-fifty chance that he'd be there. His hearing wasn't the best and he refused to wear a hearing aid, so if he wasn't close to a phone or was engaged in one of his many projects, he wouldn't even hear it ring.

But when David pulled up, his grandfather's truck was in the driveway. He pulled up behind it and then walked up to the front door and rang the bell. When no one answered, he knocked and then got nervous when there was still no response. Gramps didn't have the best heart. He took medicine to keep it under control, but sometimes when he'd been doing really well for a while, he would stop taking his medicine, or wouldn't rush to refill one of his prescriptions when he ran out, thinking that because he was feeling fine, he didn't need the medicine anymore.

Two visits to the ER straightened him out. The first time, he'd ignored getting his Coumadin levels adjusted. He was supposed to check in every few weeks to have his blood levels checked and that would determine what dose of blood thinner he'd need. Gramps loved spinach, and after learning how to cook it himself, he went on a bit of a spinach binge, having large amounts for several weeks in a row, which resulted in his arm turning black.

As it turned out, spinach reacted with the Coumadin in a strange way, but if he'd had his blood checked, they would have been able to easily adjust his dose to compensate. The second visit was when he ran out of all his meds at once and decided to go without since he felt absolutely fine. Of course, his doctor read him the riot act, reminding him that the only reason he felt fine was because of the meds. That last visit scared him enough that he stopped fooling around with his meds. At least David thought he had learned his lesson.

David walked around the house, peeking in the living room first. Maybe his grandfather had the stereo blasting or the TV so loud that hadn't heard the bell or his knock at the door. It wouldn't be the first time. But no, the living room was empty. He walked around to the back and found his grandfather high up on a ladder, changing a light bulb.

"Gramps, what are you doing? Let me do that." His grandfather should not be climbing ladders; his balance wasn't the steadiest and if he slipped and fell there was an excellent chance that he'd break something.

"I can change a light bulb." He gave the bulb one final twist, then carefully backed down the ladder. "See, all set."

"I can see that. I wish you'd call me though for stuff like this. It only takes me two seconds to run over here."

"Thank you, but I'm not exactly feeble yet. What brings you out here anyway?"

"I was just driving by and thought I'd stop in and say hello."

His grandfather stared at him for a moment, weighing what he'd just said. "Hmmm, all right then, why don't you come in and sit for a bit. Have a piece of Lucy's Banana nut bread. She dropped a loaf off earlier. She even added chocolate chips, just for me 'cuz I once mentioned how much I like it that way." Lucy was one of several lady friends that liked to spoil Gramps. They'd met in a bereavement support group shortly after Grams died. Lucy was a few years younger, and like Gramps had been married for many years before her husband, Lou, passed away after a long illness. Lucy lived nearby and the two of them played bingo together every week.

"What can I get you to drink? Coffee, soda, beer?" Gramps held the refrigerator door wide open and was fishing around, looking for something.

"You have beer?" Gramps didn't drink beer.

"There's a can or two buried in here somewhere. Alan left a few cans behind after one of our card games, maybe a year or so ago." He pulled out a can of Orange soda for himself.

"What kind of beer?" David asked, more out of curiosity than interest.

"Let's see. Keystone Light."

"I'll have what you're having." Gramps poured two glasses of soda and then cut two thick slices of banana bread and stuck them in the microwave for twenty seconds.

"This makes all the difference. Melts the chocolate just enough. Tell me what you think." He handed a plate to David and they sat down at the kitchen breakfast bar. David took a bite of the bread, which was warm, soft and chock-full of walnuts and gooey chocolate.

"Good stuff. So, what's going on with Lucy? Are you going to marry her?" he teased.

"I'm not marrying anybody! I was married to your grandmother for over fifty years. I'm not doing that again. Besides, Lucy and I are just friends. She's good company."

"How long did you date Grams before you decided to get married? How well did you know her?"

"I knew all I needed to know after three dates. We'd gone dancing on our third date and out for ice cream afterward. That's what we did in those days. Not like today. I came home from that date and told my mother 'I'm going to marry that girl.' And I did, less than a year later. There was never any doubt in my mind that she was the one for me." Gramps took a big bite of his banana bread, washed it down with a gulp of orange soda and then said, "Why do you ask?"

"Just curious." They ate their bread and discussed the Red Sox for a bit. And then David changed the subject to the real reason he was there.

"Gramps, have you been following the news the past few days?"

"You mean all the garbage they're saying about Lauren and that boy?"

"Yeah."

"You don't think there's a lick of truth to it, right?"

"No, of course not!"

"So, what's the problem then?" Gramps polished off the last crumb on his plate and reached to cut another. "Want one more?"

"Sure, why not?" David pushed his plate over. Like his grandfather, he had a hard time saying no to anything with chocolate in it.

"I know there's nothing to it and I know Lauren. But, it's been stressful for her and the media has a way of twisting things. If I didn't know her, I'd be inclined to lean toward thinking there must be something to it—where there's smoke there's fire and all that. Plus, you know how a lot of people are; if they see it in print they think it has to be true."

"Your grandmother was like that," Gramps agreed.

"I'm afraid that it could get worse if they keep digging. Do you remember the Nancy Hines murder? It was over twenty years ago."

"'Course I do. It wasn't one of our finer moments."

"Do you remember the kids involved; the three who confessed?"

"You know two of 'em."

"Two?"

"Our assistant Sheriff, Jake, for one, and your partner Billy. The other was a girl, Melissa Hopkins. Tiny little thing, with big eyes and real short hair. What do they call that?" He snapped his fingers. "Pixie cut, that's it. Her family moved away shortly after. Can't say that I blame them."

David was trying to wrap his head around all this.

"Jake, well that actually does make sense. He told me years ago that something had happened to him when he was a teenager that inspired him to go into law enforcement. He didn't go into a lot of details, just said something about being charged with something he didn't do and that it worked out in the end, but that the process needed fixing. He never talks about it."

"Why relive the past?" Gramps was always a big believer in moving forward.

"But Billy—that's a surprise."

"Don't see why it should be. You know Billy grew up here and is the same age as you and Jake. They've been friends for years too. Like I said—good kids. They've done well for themselves."

David debated for a moment whether or not to tell his Grandfather about Lauren, but then remembered that was the main reason for his visit.

"So, I learned something interesting on the ride home from Maine."

"What's that?"

"You know that girl you mentioned, Melissa Hopkins? Well that was Lauren." He explained about the divorce and the name change.

"Interesting. Her hair's long now and maybe a little lighter than I remembered and of course, many years have passed. No wonder no one recognized her. Smart of her to change her name. Those media fools would have had a field day with that nonsense."

The thought had crossed David's mind as well. "Any advice you might have for dealing with this?"

"Sure. Tell Lauren not to talk to anyone. Less said the better."

20

Lauren was relieved to see that there were no media vans outside her door Monday morning. She was able to take her normal route to Starbucks, and armed with an extra-large black coffee she pulled into the school parking lot and was thrilled to see that not even a single TV van was waiting out front.

"I feel guilty for saying this, but I'm actually a little thankful for the drug shootout in Dorchester," she said to Amy who had stopped by her office to see how the weekend went.

"I know. You're old news now and at least the Dorchester thing was drug pushers killing other drug pushers. Gang warfare, and good riddance if you ask me. So, how did you like The Road's End?"

"It was amazing." She told Amy how they'd been upgraded to the honeymoon suite.

"That's the room we got too. They knew it was our anniversary."

They compared notes for the next few minutes then agreed to meet up at the end of the day for a visit to the local Target. Lauren wanted to check out their curtain selection. She had the measurements of the windows in the new house they were going to be moving into and wanted to see if anything at Target might work. She'd heard they had a decent selection of inexpensive curtains and David wasn't going to be home until later that night. He had a lot of work to catch up on after losing the afternoon golfing on Friday.

Lauren thought back to the car ride home. David had taken her news relatively well. She could understand his initial hesitation, not understanding why she hadn't told him about her past before, but she meant what she said. She didn't want to dredge up the past. She had moved on and had permanently closed that chapter of her life. Melissa Hopkins did not exist anymore.

She did feel a little guilty about not telling David everything though. It just seemed like too much information to dump on him at once, about who the other two were, especially considering how close he and Jake were. It was a little surprising that he wasn't aware of Jake's involvement, although she supposed it was something that Jake didn't enjoy revisiting either.

She played with her hair for a few minutes. It was a nervous habit she had, twisting her hair over and over while she was mulling something over. Often, she didn't even realize she was doing it. Out of the corner of her eye, she caught a glimpse of the ends, which were looking a little split. She was overdue for a cut and color. She colored it regularly, mostly to hide the gray that was creeping in along her hairline. She also added golden highlights every few months, which brought her light brown hair to a dark shimmery blonde. It was lighter now than it had been when she was a teenager and it was amazing how different she looked with long hair.

She kept it long because she liked it that way, and also because she had wanted to make sure that Jake or Billy didn't recognize her. Not that she really cared about either of them knowing who she really was, but if they recognized her, then others were likely to as well. Then the buzz would start and the past dredged up and people might look at her differently. Especially now. If this information surfaced, there was no doubt that her job could be in jeopardy.

Lauren pushed the troubling thoughts away and forced herself to focus on the lesson plans for the day. Before she knew it, the day was done and she was in her office wrapping things up. Her phone rang and she assumed it was Amy. She picked up the phone and said, "I'll be ready in a few minutes."

"Lauren?" The somewhat familiar male voice was most definitely not Amy.

"Sorry, I thought you were someone else."

"It's Jake. We need to talk. Can I stop by the house later tonight? Maybe around seven? Oh, and Lauren, it might be best if David isn't there. If you think he'll be there I can come another time, maybe a little earlier, before he gets home?"

"Sure. I'm going out with Amy for a little bit, but I'll be home by seven. David called earlier to say he'll be working late. I don't expect him before eight or so."

She put the phone down, grabbed her stuff and started

walking towards Amy's office, fighting the urge to twirl her hair, which she couldn't have done anyway as her hands were full. The only thing she could figure was that Jake must have somehow figured out who she was.

The rumor about Target turned out to be true. They did have surprisingly nice curtains and in colors that Lauren loved. She bought a mix of baby blue, a gorgeous barely-there green and buttery cream. Jake was waiting in his car outside her condo when she pulled up at ten minutes to seven.

"I know, I'm early," he said as she walked towards his car. "Want some help with those bags?" Lauren handed him the two overstuffed bags she was carrying and ran back to her car to get the other two.

"Thanks," she said as they walked to her door. Once they were in, Lauren dropped the bags in the dining room and then offered Jake a drink.

"I wouldn't say no to a beer." She got him a Sam Adams out of the fridge, poured it into a tall glass and then poured herself a glass of chardonnay. She had a feeling she was going to want a drink for this conversation.

They sat at the dining room table across from each other and Lauren tried to fight back a case of the nerves. This was just Jake, David's best friend. Yes, he was also a cop, but she hadn't done anything wrong.

"I got an interesting phone call today," Jake began. "It was an anonymous call, but I think it was someone in the media looking to see how I'd react."

Lauren took a sip of her wine and waited for him to continue.

"They told me that I should look into your past and into mine. Then they got more specific and told me exactly where to go, to the False Confession case as it's known. You may have heard of that case, about twenty years ago? It was all over the news." He held her gaze then, waiting for her reaction, but Lauren forced herself to stay calm.

"Yes, I'm familiar with it."

"I didn't understand where they were going with this. Why they wanted me to dredge up that old case, but they wouldn't say anything else. Just wished me 'happy hunting' and said they'd be in touch. At first, I just thought they were fishing, but after I spent some time on this, and connected a few dots, I realized that they knew exactly what they were doing and I suspect it's just a matter of time before this goes public. I think you know that would be a very bad thing."

"Yes. I agree," Lauren said simply. It would be horrific.

"My take on it is that it might be a warning, a push for us to move faster on this case and find whoever did this. If I do, then they won't have to dredge up the past, which Billy and I would certainly prefer. People don't connect us with that old case any longer, we've both moved on and found success here."

"I was always a little surprised that neither of you ever recognized me." Lauren admitted.

"I can see it now that I'm looking for it, and it's funny, because I did mention to David when you first started dating that you looked familiar, but I could never put my finger on where I knew you from."

PAMELA M. KELLEY

"So, how did you connect the dots?"

"It was simple really. I just looked at everyone involved and tracked where they went over the years. It wasn't difficult to see that your family moved out west, your parents filed for divorce, and then both you and your mother officially changed your names. There's a paper trail for that kind of thing. Legal documents filed, etc. It took me less than an hour to find you."

That was a sobering thought. Lauren set down the glass of wine she'd been holding.

"You understand why we did it though? Why the name-change?"

"Yeah, I get it. You wanted to move forward, leave that particular piece of history buried well in your past. What I don't get, though, is why you came back here of all places?"

"I don't really understand myself. I just always loved Waverly, always felt like this was home. When I saw the posting for a new teacher, it seemed like a sign. I thought enough time had passed that it wouldn't matter. That no one would recognize me and I could do two things at once, come home and start fresh here."

"I wanted to see you without David here because I didn't know if he was aware of your past, or of my involvement? I'm guessing probably not or he would have said something. I didn't hide it from him. I always told him I got into police work because of an incident in my childhood, but I never got too specific. Like you, I didn't want to go back there."

"Oddly enough, I just told him yesterday, on the drive back from Maine."

"How did he take it?"

"He wished I'd told him sooner. But in the end, I think he understood why I never mentioned it. Like you, I don't want to dredge up the past. Of course it would be totally different if our confessions hadn't been overturned." David had been very quiet since they got home. She sensed that he needed some time to process everything that she'd told him.

"I know. It's crossed my mind more than once how different our lives might have been if it wasn't for Billy's Dad." Jake polished off the rest of the beer, then asked, "Did you tell him who the other two kids were? It must have floored him to find out it was me and Billy."

"He didn't ask and I didn't mention it. If he'd asked, of course I would have told him, but it seemed like enough at that point. I'm sure he'll ask, though."

"His ears must be ringing," Jake commented as the front door opened and David walked in and his eyes narrowed as he saw the two of them sitting in the dining room, drinking.

"What's going on?" He dropped his briefcase by the door and walked past them into the kitchen.

"Jake, do you need another?" He grabbed himself a beer and then another for Jake who answered the question by handing over his empty bottle. David opened them both, handed one to Jake and then sat at the table.

"So, Lauren, Jake, how are things?" His tone was pleasant, but his eyes were clearly saying, "What the hell is going on?"

Lauren answered first. "David, Jake came by to discuss something." She hesitated and looked at Jake for a moment trying to figure out where to begin. To her relief, Jake jumped in. "Lauren and I were discussing the old False Confession case, and she mentioned that she'd just told you about it yesterday."

David nodded and said, "It was quite a story."

"Well, I don't think she told you the whole story, about who the other two kids were?"

"She didn't," he confirmed.

"Well, you know how I told you that I was motivated to join the police force after an incident in my childhood? Well that was it. I was one of the other two kids, and you actually know the other one as well, it's...."

"Billy," David said matter-of-factly and both Lauren and Jake looked at him in surprise and then exchanged glances.

"You knew about Billy?" Lauren asked.

"My grandfather filled me in. I stopped by his place on the way home, wondering what he remembered about the case. He was actually on vacation that week, so wasn't involved in any of the interrogations, but was in the thick of things with the aftermath. He said it wasn't one of the department's prouder moments."

"I'm sorry I never told you about this before," Jake began.

"I get it," David assured him. "And you did sort of tell me about it. What was important was that it inspired you to become who you are. The details don't matter as much."

He smiled at Lauren and she relaxed a little. She hadn't realized how worried she'd been all day wondering if David was really okay with this.

"The main reason for this meeting though, was about a phone call I received regarding the Eric Armstrong case." He filled David in on what he'd told Lauren earlier.

"You have no idea who the caller was?" David asked.

"None. The call was traced to one of those pre-paid cell phones that anyone can buy at a convenience store. They're anonymous, no trail to follow."

"How likely do you think it is that this will end up on the front page?" Lauren asked.

"Unfortunately, I don't think it's a matter of if so much as when. If we're far along in the case with another suspect, it will likely be a non-issue, in the news for a few days, then quickly fading away. But, if this drags on and we're still not getting anywhere and we have no potential suspects other than Lauren, who at this point is barely considered a 'person of interest', then it could be a huge issue. It would raise all kinds of questions about Lauren's credibility with the name change. They'll slant it to make it look like she's trying to hide something."

"Are there any other leads? Have you made any progress?" David asked.

"No, and not for lack of trying either. Thing is, we don't really have any kind of a motive for this. He had no enemies that anyone was aware of. For all we know, it could be some kind of sick random killing. We don't like to think of those things, but they can happen anywhere, even in small towns where you think you're perfectly safe."

"Like what happened to that woman and her daughter in New Hampshire," Lauren said with a shudder. She'd barely slept the night that story was on the news. A forty-two year-old nurse and mother was asleep in bed, her daughter was asleep in her own bedroom down the hall, and the husband was out of town on business.

At 4:00 a.m., four teenage boys broke into the house. Two of them used a machete and a carving knife to kill the mother while she slept and attacked the daughter as well, leaving her for dead. The killing was a thrill-kill, and the teens chose the house because it was in a quiet part of town and the most secluded house on the street. Ironically, the family had recently moved to the area from the city because they wanted a smaller, safer environment.

"We will catch whoever did this," Jake said with conviction. "This kind of thing just doesn't happen in Waverly. Not on my watch anyway."

21

David went into work early the next day. Even though he'd been made partner, his workload hadn't lightened a bit—not that he was complaining. As much as he disliked spending time with the guy, it had already paid off; there was a message on his machine from Randy; he had a nice referral for him, a friend of his wife, Sharon's, parents. Most of his new business was from referrals now that he had a good base of established clients.

He still did his fair share of networking though, getting his face out there in the community, going to Chamber of Commerce events, things like that. Lauren had even encouraged him to start going to church more often, to get more involved. He'd never been a big churchgoer, but he did like the idea of doing some volunteer work. He'd been thinking about getting involved for years, and Lauren had given him the nudge he'd needed. Plus, he knew she liked having him go with her.

His first volunteer mission was for the upcoming weekend. Their church participated along with other local churches in providing shelter and food for homeless men each night for a week. These overnights of hospitality rotated amongst six churches. David, along with several other chaperones, would be sleeping in the Parish hall Saturday night at the church along with a dozen or so homeless men. Lauren and a few of the women would be there earlier in the evening to prepare and serve hot meals. David was thinking about how awful it must be to be homeless in the winter when Chuck tapped on his door. The door was half-closed but he knew it was Chuck by the impeccable shine on his shoes.

Every few days, Chuck stopped by the train station on his way into work and visited the shoeshine station. He was meticulous about his appearance, wearing only the best suits and keeping his blonde hair gelled to perfection. David suspected that he also got manicures, as his hands were in better condition than Lauren's, and she got her nails done at least once, if not twice a month.

"Come on in. What's up?" David waved for Chuck to enter and have a seat, but he remained standing.

"I won't keep you long. I just wanted to see if you're still up for dinner tonight with the wives. We were thinking of Solstice. If that works for you, I'll have Mary make reservations."

"Um, sure. Lauren loves Solstice." David did too, but he'd completely forgotten about dinner tonight. When they gave him the promotion, Billy and Chuck also said that they wanted to go out and celebrate properly. He'd have to call Lauren and remind her in case she'd forgotten too.

"All right then. We'll catch up around seven for a drink at the bar first." Chuck was down the hall a moment later. They hadn't done dinner together as a group for several years, before he met Lauren actually, now that he thought about it. They'd met Lauren, of course, at the annual Christmas party and occasional visits to the office, but had never had a conversation of any length.

This could be interesting, especially once the cocktails started flowing. Billy and Chuck did enjoy their cocktails. Who was he kidding—he did too, though he usually didn't go too overboard. Billy, on the other hand, occasionally entered 'BillyLand', a nickname David came up with in college to refer to the point where Billy crossed over from being slightly inebriated to silly, and often manically, drunk. He didn't get that way often, and when he did, a good time was usually had by all, because Billy was generally a very happy drunk. Chuck, on the other hand, wasn't.

Chuck was more serious and reserved than Billy to begin with, and a few drinks usually loosened him up, making him more social and fun to be around. He never crossed the line though, the way Billy did. Chuck was always in complete control; he was very concerned about how others viewed him and prided himself on being a polished professional.

Billy was an open book, always the life of the party and wore his emotions on his sleeve. Chuck was much more private and low key. David realized that he didn't know a whole lot about Chuck except for the obvious, that he was a great investment manager and adored his wife Kate. He rubbed his temple and glanced at the stack of papers on his desk, which was quite a bit smaller than when he arrived this morning.

If he kept focused, he'd be able to get through everything and maybe even get a head start on tomorrow's work in case he needed to come in a little later. He smiled to himself, already planning ahead to have a good time tonight and perhaps would need a little extra shut-eye in the morning. He picked up the phone to call Lauren and remind her they were on for seven.

22

Jake stared at his computer screen. He wasn't at all happy with the progress they'd made on the Eric Armstrong case. They had no suspects and even Lauren was about to be completely cleared as a person of interest. There wasn't a shred of real evidence to connect her to anything. Just a bit of hearsay and rumors of an affair with a student, which so far had not been corroborated in any way. The computer records from the school came back clean. They'd combed Lauren's email program looking for any correspondence between her and Eric. There was none. The only time his name was even there was in Outlook, on the calendar page, as a recurring appointment, "Counseling Session with Eric" every Monday afternoon. That fit with what she'd told them, and the school psychologist, Betty, vouched for her. Lauren was approaching squeaky-clean status. He was glad to see that, for her sake and for David's. But still, it really didn't help his case any. He was considering sending one of the officers back out to the parent's to make sure they hadn't missed anything when his cell phone rang.

"Jake?" He didn't recognize the number on his caller ID, but the voice sounded familiar.

"You got him."

"Ted Bishop here, David's grandfather. You got a minute?"

"Of course. I didn't recognize your number."

"David got me a cell phone—one of those fancy iPhone things—and programmed in a bunch of numbers."

"That's great."

"So, the reason I'm calling is, I think you might want to come talk to my neighbor, Alan. He's here having coffee at my place. We got to talking and well, I think you might want to hear what he has to say. It's about that Eric Armstrong case. He might have seen something."

"I'll be right there." Jake grabbed his coat and half-full cup of coffee and headed out. David's grandfather was up there in years, but he was still sharper than most people were, and Jake knew how well thought of he was in the department.

Ten minutes later, he was sitting in the kitchen with David's grandfather and his friend Alan who lived across the street.

"You sure you don't want some of Lucy's Carrot Cake? It makes for a delicious breakfast." He and Alan were enjoying large slices of it along with their coffee.

"No, thanks. I'm all set. Had an egg sandwich on the way in." He took another sip of his coffee, which was barely lukewarm at this point.

"So Alan, tell Jake what you told me earlier. Don't leave anything out."

"Right. Well I work part-time down at the new cemetery." Older folks called Greystone Cemetery 'new', even though it was almost twenty years old. Still, it was the youngest cemetery in town. "And you know how it backs up to Pine Pond? Well, at the end of my shift, usually around three in the afternoon, if the weather is decent enough I'll often take a walk down there and see if the fish are biting. I always have my fishing gear in the back of the truck, just in case.

Jake nodded, and after swallowing a huge bite of carrot cake, Alan continued. "Well, I was telling Ed here that it was a real nice afternoon yesterday; sun was shining, it wasn't too cold and there was no wind, so I decided to check things out and settle in for an hour or two see if I might get lucky and land a striper or two."

"You catch stripers down there?" Jake was surprised.

"Well, no. I haven't actually yet. But I think it's possible."

"Hurry it up, get to the good stuff. Jake doesn't have all day here. He's a busy man, right Jake?" He winked at Jake and Jake realized he was enjoying this.

"Yeah, well like I said, I was going to settle in for a bit and was just about to set my chair up when out of the corner of my eye, something flashed in the sun and got my attention. I walked over to investigate, and sticking out of a pile of leaves was a shiny golf club. I thought that a little odd as the country club is clear on the other side of the lake. I remembered what Ed had said about how the murder weapon of that Armstrong kid might be a golf club so I knew not to touch it. I kicked the leaves away from the club head and sure enough, it looked as if there was something unusual. At first it just looked like dirt, but when I leaned over and got a closer look, I wondered if it might be dried blood."

"Is it here? Did you bring it home?" Jake felt a shiver of excitement. Finally, they might have a real lead if this was actually the murder weapon.

"Hell, no. I wasn't about to touch the thing. I know better than that. I've listened to Ed's stories over the years and I wasn't going to be blamed for screwing things up. I left it right where I found it. Well, I did kick a few more leaves over it, so the shiny part is covered, but I know exactly where it is. I can take you there."

"Great, let's go. I'll drive if you guys want to ride with me." Alan's eyes lit up and Jake smiled. "Why don't you ride shotgun? Let Ed see how the back seat feels." No matter what their age, most guys got a thrill out of riding around in a cop car.

Fifteen minutes later, Alan was leading them down the path to his favorite fishing spot. "It's right over there," he said as they got closer to the water. "Good, it's still here." About an inch of the club handle was all that was visible, the rest of the club was smothered in leaves. Jake pulled a glove out of his pocket, put it on, brushed the leaves away and then carefully lifted the club to get a closer look at the dark brown smudges on the club head.

"What do you think?" Alan asked. "Is it blood? Do you think it's the murder weapon?"

"That's not dirt," Ed said matter-of-factly.

"Certainly looks like dried blood to me," Jake said. "We'll

have to get it into the lab and run some tests, see if we can get any finger prints off the club and a match from the blood."

"Alan, you done good." Ed gave Alan a hard slap on the back.

"Thanks. You were the one that made the connection though, and said to call it into Jake.

"Thank you, both of you." Jake said. "If this is the murder weapon it could be just the break we needed. To be perfectly frank, we don't have much of anything else to go on."

23

David checked his watch; it was only quarter past six. They had plenty of time to meet everyone at Solstice by seven. He'd called Lauren earlier to remind her about the dinner tonight and she said it was on her calendar and she was looking forward to it. She even knew what she was going to wear. She'd dropped one of her favorite dresses off a few days ago at the dry cleaner and asked David if he wouldn't mind picking it up on his way home as it was a few doors down from his office. Since it was so early, he reached into the refrigerator and grabbed a beer. The restaurant they were going to was only a five minute drive away, and knowing Lauren as he did, she wouldn't be downstairs for a least a half-hour.

He wasn't looking forward to tonight. He'd been feeling edgy all day. The beer was definitely helping to calm his nerves a little. It bothered him that he was feeling this way. He told himself it was ridiculous. So what if Billy did recognize Lauren finally? They were just kids back then and neither one did anything wrong. Still, he couldn't shake a disturbing sense of foreboding. He took the last sip of his beer just as Lauren came down the stairs, looking drop dead gorgeous in a long silky midnight blue dress that made her hazel eyes seem more blue and dazzling.

"You look amazing."

"Thank you. You look pretty good yourself." All David had done to get ready was to give himself a quick shave and swap his tie for a dressier blue-gray one that Lauren had picked out for him.

They hit a little traffic, but still made it to the restaurant a minute or two before seven. Chuck and his wife Katy were already enjoying a drink at the bar and Chuck lifted his glass to wave them over.

"What are you having? I've got this one," he said as the bartender came over to take their drink order.

"Lauren, what are you having?" David asked.

"Chardonnay, please."

"I'll go with a dirty martini with plenty of extra olives. Thanks."

"Make that Grey Goose," Chuck added as the bartender was about to grab the house vodka. He and Katy were both drinking martinis as well. Chuck always raved about Grey Goose vodka, said it was the best and the smoothest. David didn't drink vodka as often as beer, so he wasn't as familiar with the nuances among them. He took a sip when Chuck handed him the drink and it was pretty smooth, he had to admit.

"Billy called and said they were running about twenty

minutes late." Katy told them as they settled at a high-topped table in the corner. Katy sold real estate and had one of the busiest offices in town. She and Chuck had recently celebrated their first wedding anniversary.

"I can't believe it's already been over a year. It seems like just a short time ago when I was running around getting ready for our wedding like you are now." She smiled. "We're both looking forward to the wedding."

"The two week countdown has started," Lauren said then asked, "So how did you and Chuck meet? I always love to hear people's 'how we met' stories.

"He walked in the office one day looking to buy a house, and it was my turn to take a walk-in. It's funny too, because friends had been saying for years that they thought my job would be a great way to meet people, but I had never met anyone I wanted to date until Chuck showed up. Of course, that was almost ten years ago, and then we were engaged for five years. I think my mom just about gave up hope that the wedding would actually happen."

"So, I'm a little slow. What can I say?" Chuck smiled and then added, "I think your mom would agree the wedding itself was worth the wait." David caught Lauren's eye and smiled. He'd told her about Chuck's wedding as an example of what he didn't want. He had never been to such an over-the-top wedding. He didn't want to imagine what it must have cost Chuck.

They had six hundred people in attendance easily. All of Chuck's clients were invited and it seemed like almost the entire town was there. Plus Katy was from a large family. She had eight siblings and loads of cousins. No expense was spared. The hotel was the most expensive in town and was on a huge cliff overlooking the water with spectacular views. Chuck had booked and paid for the entire hotel that night, all one hundred twenty rooms. There was a ten-piece band and the food was decadent. There was even a caviar and vodka bar. And that was just what David could remember. A good time was definitely had by all.

"Here they are!" Chuck said as Billy and Julie walked through the door. They joined them and Chuck waved down the bartender and asked him to bring two more martinis. Julie pulled a chair over and sat next to Lauren and Billy sat across the table between David and Chuck. Lauren glanced at Billy and tried to see the boy she'd known so many years ago.

There were hints of him, but if not for his name, she realized she probably wouldn't have recognized him. Like many men his age, Billy's hair had thinned, receded, and had quite a bit of gray. He'd never been one of the more athletic guys, always had more of a slight, leaner frame. But now he had a generous round belly and a slight double chin.

It wasn't all that noticeable though, as the neatly trimmed mustache and goatee hid most of it and the dark brown, almost black hair gave his face a slightly dangerous quality.

Julie noticed her looking at Billy's face. "Can you believe he grew that thing again? I can't stand it. Told him it makes him look like Lucifer, evil and scary. Plus it scratches."

"I don't think it looks that bad," Lauren said politely. Billy overheard her and smiled.

"Thank you. See, Julie? Some people like it."

"They don't have to live with it," she said teasingly and Lauren saw that she obviously didn't mind that much.

"It's just for the winter," Billy explained. "As soon as spring comes, I shave it right off."

Their waitress came over at that point, said their table was ready and led them into the main dining room. Lauren had only been to Solstice once before. It was wonderful, but a bit pricey, and she mentally put it into the category of 'special occasion only' restaurant. Their table was a large round one, which would make for easy conversation and was right next to an enormous gas fireplace that was glowing cheerily.

They decided to order a few bottles of wine, an Italian Prosecco, to go with the seafood appetizers of Oysters Rockefeller, Shrimp Cocktail and tuna tartare and then a rich Cabernet Sauvignon with the entree, since most of them had decided on red meat.

Julie was sitting on Lauren's left and while they were sipping their glasses of bubbly Prosecco, they happened to both glance across the table at the same time and saw Katy shoot Chuck a look of fury.

"I can't believe you went ahead and booked that fishing trip for the same weekend my parents and sisters are coming to town. They'll be so insulted if you're not there. Can't you change it?"

"No, and we can talk about this at home. My trip has been set for months. Maybe your family should reschedule."

"They already bought their tickets." By now, they had everyone's attention.

"No one wants to hear this. Like I said, we can talk about

this at home. Oh look, the appetizers are here." Their waitress set down platters of food and the topic of conversation immediately switched to the food in front of them. Lauren squeezed some lemon over her oysters Rockefeller and took a bite. This was a dish she'd always loved, a baked oyster topped with spinach and a creamy, cheesy sauce with a hint of Pernod. Their version was divine and she closed her eyes for a moment, savoring the flavor.

Julie brought her attention back to Chuck and Katy who were obviously still annoyed with each other. "They've been fighting like this more and more," she whispered. "Maybe there was a reason it took them so long to get married. Chuck's an odd duck though. I'm not sure who else would suit him as well as she does. She puts up with a lot."

"What do you mean?" Lauren really didn't know any of them well enough to know how things were with their marriages. She and David had always seen them in passing, the occasional short conversation at various parties; it wasn't as if they hung out at each other's houses or even really ran in the same circles. Not yet anyway.

David had mentioned that Julie and Katy were active in a local women's group, sort of like the Junior League, and that maybe Lauren might want to get involved. It was more like a social group from what Billy said and was by invitation only which meant it was so exclusive that being a part of this group was in big demand. Lauren thought it sounded a bit silly and a little cliquish, but agreed to keep an open mind.

"Well, he's always been a bit of a loner, does his own thing. He does this all the time and it drives Katy crazy. She swears he seems to do it on purpose, always out of town for events that she has scheduled. Billy says he's just absent-minded, head in the clouds."

"That would be annoying." Lauren was grateful that David was even more organized and on top of things than she was. He blamed it on having OCD and needing things to be orderly. Lauren assured him that it wasn't a bad thing and actually, since they'd been almost living together, his OCD had rubbed off on her in a good way as she had a tendency to be a bit of a pack rat. Staying with David now helped her make sure she threw things out before they turned into clutter.

"So, did David mention that we want you to join the Group?" Julie asked.

"He did. I don't know much about it though."

"Oh, it's great. You'll love it. It's a fantastic group of women. We do some really important things, fund-raising events for local charities, such as the October Masquerade gala at the Sycamore mansion; you know, that glorious museum on the waterfront?" Lauren nodded and Julie continued, "We had over four hundred people attend last year at over one hundred and fifty dollars a ticket! With proceeds from ticket sales and the silent auction, we raised an enormous amount of money for the local food pantries."

"That's wonderful." Lauren was impressed. She'd done some volunteering at the food pantry at her church in California and knew how important every extra dollar was to make sure enough food got to the people who needed it.

"Of course, we are mostly a social club," Julie admitted. "We meet once a month at a different member's house. Some people bring appetizers or wine, and we talk business for a few minutes, then drink wine, enjoy the food and have a good time."

"That sounds fun. I'd love to join you." Lauren liked the idea of getting to know more people in town. Although she was friendly with many of the parents of her children and had plenty of casual acquaintances, Amy was really her only close friend. In California, she'd been part of a neighborhood women's book group and loved it. That had been more of a social group as well. There was always a book to be read, but the discussion never lasted more than a few minutes. The rest of the time was spent catching up with each other over cocktails and munchies. It would be nice to be a part of something like that again.

"Great, I'll bring it up at our next meeting and will get an email off to you after that with details on where we'll be meeting next."

Across the table, Billy was in the middle of a story about one of his clients. His face was flushed and his arms were gesturing animatedly as he talked.

"My husband never shuts up," Julie said with amusement. "He's always been like this—non-stop chatter. He told me when we were dating that his Dad once tried to bribe him to be quiet; said he'd give him ten dollars if he didn't say a word for ten minutes. He couldn't do it."

"David's very much the opposite," Lauren said. "He's more of an observer, taking it all in."

"Probably why they get along so well. They complement each other. David is Billy's straight man. Not that Billy's all that funny really, but you know what I mean."

Lauren nodded and then asked, "How did you and Billy meet?" She knew they'd been married for years.

"We were college sweethearts. I was dating one of Billy's fraternity brothers the first half of freshman year, and Billy and I got to be close friends. When Jason and I broke up, I just started hanging out even more with Billy. Next thing we knew we were dating and here we are."

"You seem like such a great couple, like you have the whole marriage thing figured out." Lauren hoped that she and David would still be as close after they'd been married as long as Julie and Billy had. She felt pretty sure that they would.

"Appearances can be deceiving," Julie said with the slightest edge to her voice and Lauren immediately turned her attention back to what she was saying.

"Really?" Lauren was surprised to hear that. The two of them seemed almost too perfect.

They paused for a moment as the appetizers were cleared, the entrees arrived and the wine, a luscious Groth Cabernet, was poured. Julie took a sip of wine and checked to make sure Billy was still deep in conversation before continuing.

"He has a bit of a dark side," she admitted. "This is happy Billy, all outgoing and a little manic even. What most people never see is the other Billy, the one that is really down and almost depressed. That Billy mopes around the house and goes off for hours by himself, and when he's in one of those moods, I've learned to just stay out of his way."

"Does he take medicine for it?" Lauren asked. What Julie was describing sounded like manic-depressive behavior, maybe even bi-polar. Over the years, she'd seen it in some of her students and the ones who were diagnosed and treated with meds generally did very well.

"No, but he should. I've been trying to talk him into seeing someone for years. He doesn't think there's anything wrong."

Lauren glanced over at Billy and found it hard to picture him any other way than how she'd always seen him, like this—animated, upbeat and always the life of the party.

He caught them glancing his way and smiled. "What are you two up to? You look like you're plotting something serious. Is there a big sale coming up at Beaulah's that you don't want us to know about?" Beaulah's was the most expensive boutique in town. Lauren only shopped there when they were having a sale and even then, it was an indulgence she couldn't really afford.

"No, honey. We were just talking recipes, about what appetizer Lauren might want to bring to her first meeting for the Waverly Women's Group."

"That's great, Lauren you'll love it. Julie's really involved in that group. They throw great parties." His eyes held a hint of mischief at that before he turned his attention back to David and Chuck and an upcoming Patriot's football game.

"Beaulah's has great shoes," Katy commented. Now that they were done with their meals, she made Chuck switch seats so she could better talk to the girls.

"Billy knows Beulah's is one of my weaknesses. I have a little room in the basement that Billy thinks is just storage, and that's where I hide new purchases if I splurge a little too much. Then I introduce one item at a time and he never notices like he would if I suddenly had a bunch of new stuff in the closet."

"Doesn't he know from the bank account statements?" Katy asked.

"Well, that's what tipped him off initially and why he still teases me about it. I have a separate account now, so when I have an 'accident' as I call it, and go a little overboard with the shopping, he'll never know and if he's in one of his black moods, I won't have to worry about dealing with it."

"That's a smart move," Katy said with admiration. Lauren wasn't so sure though. Is that what happened in a marriage— you had to hide things from each other? She hoped it would never come to that with David and her.

They arrived home a little before midnight. Billy had insisted on after dinner drinks so they'd moved back to the bar for another round. David only had one glass of port though, and he sipped it slowly while the others kept going. Lauren was still working on her second glass of Cabernet from dinner. Once her food arrived, she tended to slow down her drinking and had barely touched her first glass of wine, delicious as it was, by the time everyone was done with theirs.

Billy had noticed and insisted that she polish off what was left in the bottle, and topped off her glass. She had no idea how many drinks Billy had. He seemed the same as when the night started, maybe a little more boisterous, but not at all drunk, which was incredible given how quickly he was downing his drinks. He was on his third snifter of Grand Marnier when she and David decided to call it a night.

"Well, that was fun," she said as they walked into the condo. "We should do it again sometime."

"Katy mentioned having us over for dinner sometime in the next few weeks. Chuck didn't look overly thrilled at the idea though."

"He seems like a nice guy, but a little on the quiet side."

"Yeah, he's no social butterfly like Billy, that's for sure. Good thing he's so great with numbers and stock analysis because he's not a natural schmoozer. His clients love him though. He gets loads of referrals."

"I suppose if you're really good at what you do, that's what matters most," Lauren said.

"You're probably right on that," he agreed and started up the stairs. "I'm beat. Are you coming to bed?" Lauren could tell that he was likely to be asleep moments after his head hit the pillow. She wasn't that tired, not yet.

"I'm going to stay up for a little bit, see what's on TV."

"Okay, see you in the morning."

Lauren remembered she had a load of laundry in the dryer and went down to the basement to bring it up. She plopped the armful of clean clothes on the end of the sofa and flipped on the TV. She fished through the pile, found her favorite soft pajamas first and slipped out of her dress and into her jammies. Much more comfortable. An old Jimmy Stewart movie, "The Shop Around the Corner", had just started on one of the cable stations and she settled herself on the sofa to watch while she folded the rest of the laundry.

Her mind kept drifting as she gazed at the TV and mechanically folded everything into neat piles. She'd thought the evening had gone well enough. Julie and Katy seemed nice and she was looking forward to joining them soon at one of their group meetings. She kept thinking about their marriages and how what you saw wasn't always a true reflection on how things actually were.

She never would have guessed that Billy wasn't always the outgoing, upbeat person she knew or that Chuck was a bit of a loner. Still, in spite of it, they both seemed happy enough and secure and she knew from her own experience with her parents divorcing that there really was no such thing as an idyllic perfect marriage. There were always things bubbling under the surface that threatened to erupt from time to time, bumps in the road that needed smoothing out.

Her mother had always said that marriage was hard work, but she'd never understood that. She'd always had a vision of finding her true soul mate and living happily ever after. She still thought that person was David. They got along beautifully and since they'd been living together unofficially for the past six months, they'd rarely even argued. She couldn't imagine hiding things from David the way Julie did with Billy about her secret room. Thankfully, Lauren and David didn't have any trust issues like that to deal with.

Lauren was also relieved that the media buzz about her had died down. It hadn't even come up at dinner, and for that, she was grateful. She realized that she'd been a little on edge, dreading the conversation taking a turn in that direction. And neither Billy nor Chuck seemed to remember her from those days.

Chuck had been there that night too as he and Billy were

close friends from high school. Chuck had left earlier than the rest of them with a few other boys, so he didn't have to face the interrogation that she, Jake and Billy had been subjected to. She wondered if they ever thought much about that day and wondered what they'd think if they ever did make the connection that she'd been right there with them. That was a dinner conversation she definitely didn't care to be a part of.

She turned her attention back to the upcoming wedding and as she'd done a dozen times already, she went through her mental checklist to make sure there was nothing she had forgotten to do. Everything was all set though. She'd had a message from Nellie earlier in the day that their dresses were ready and they could stop by tomorrow after work for a final fitting to make sure everything was just right.

It wasn't going to be a large wedding, certainly nothing on the scale of what Chuck and Katy had done. Their wedding had reminded her of the show, Lifestyles of the Rich and Famous, where everything was completely luxurious and out of reach for most people. No, Lauren and David's wedding wasn't going to be anything like that. The guest list was about a fifth the size for starters, with about one hundred and twenty people, mostly close friends and family, and a handful of David's long-term clients, the ones he really felt were his friends. He didn't want his wedding to feel like a promotion for his business and Lauren agreed. They wanted it to have an intimate, special feeling.

They were holding it at the Edgewater Inn, one of the smaller hotels along the waterfront. The views weren't as spectacular as the hotel where Chuck and Katy got married, which was high on a cliff with sweeping panoramic views. Lauren preferred the view from the Inn anyway, as it was closer to town and was right on the busy harbor where there was always something to look at—sailboats in the summer and ferries and fishing boats all winter long, coming in and going out to sea.

She was most excited about the food though. Lauren didn't want people to feel boxed in by a fancy sit-down dinner. She wanted the reception to feel more like a free-flowing party. The seating would include a mix of cocktail and larger round tables. The food would be a succession of hot and cold hors d'oeuvres, a few meat carving stations, a pasta station, a raw bar, a salad table, and a sundae station for the kids and adults, And for the cake, she was going for something really fun and informal—a layered collection of assorted cupcakes, assembled to resemble a wedding cake.

Her favorite part of any wedding meal was always the hors d'oeuvres and she'd watched people fill up during cocktail hour and then leave their plates holding very expensive filet mignon or prime rib virtually untouched. This way, by having the stations, everyone was able to have whatever suited them. And the hors d'oeuvres were going to be a mix of retro favorites like pigs in a blanket and mini cheeseburgers on sticks, to more elegant selections such as tuna tartare, oysters Rockefeller and lobster fondue cups.

Lauren felt her eyes grow heavy as the stress melted away. Everything was set. Her wedding was on schedule and should go off without a hitch in exactly two weeks.

24

Jake wished that DNA results came back as quickly as they did on TV. He'd sent the club off to be processed first for DNA to see if there was a match for Eric Armstrong and if the answer was yes, they'd follow that with a fingerprint analysis. He'd asked for an expedited turnaround, but still, best-case scenario was about ten days. In the meantime, they continued to follow every lead, and re-interview people, as they often remembered something relevant on the second round, even when asked the exact same questions.

His stomach growled and his thoughts turned to lunch as the clock showed it was nearly noon. But then his phone rang and he forgot all about eating when Scott excitedly told him they had a new lead. A friend of Eric's decided to share some information he hadn't disclosed previously. He'd agreed to come in for further questioning and Scott said they'd be in the office any minute.

Less than ten minutes later Angie, at the front desk, rang to tell Jake that Scott and Danny were waiting for him in interrogation room B. Before he entered the room, Jake stopped in the observation area, adjacent to the room. Scott was sitting at a small table across from Danny Wells, a gawky, pimply-faced former classmate of Eric's. The table was empty except for a can of ginger ale in front of Danny, who looked a little uncomfortable and nervous to be there; but that was normal for anyone sitting in an interrogation room. Nothing unusual jumped out at him, so Jake headed into the room.

Scott jumped up to introduce him, "Danny, this is Jake McPhee, our assistant sheriff. He's going to want to ask you a few questions as well."

"Danny, nice to meet you, and thanks for coming in." Jake wanted to put the boy at ease, so he'd open up with them. He and Scott sat down across from Danny and Scott began.

"Danny, you mentioned that in addition to his hours at the club, Eric had picked up a side job?"

"Yeah, one of the new members liked the way he took care of his car for him when he was on valet. Guy drives a sweet sports car, real expensive and he liked that Eric babied it and made sure it was right out front so it'd be ready in a flash. It was also the most visible spot. I think the guy really liked that too."

"Who is this guy?" Jake asked.

"He just moved here a few months back. Randy Sykes. The guy's like a multi-millionaire or something."

"So what kind of job did he offer Eric?"

"He had a couple of big parties coming up at his house

and asked if Eric wanted to handle the valet work; said he could bring a helper as well. So he brought me."

"How did it go?" Jake asked.

"Well, the first party went off smooth as can be and we made a nice chunk of cash from it; the money Randy paid us, plus plenty of tips from the guests. It was a good gig. Randy said he was real pleased. He wasn't so happy after the next party though."

"What was different about the next party?" Jake looked up from his notepad and paid careful attention to Danny's facial expressions. He could hear from the change in his voice that this part of the story made him uncomfortable.

"Well, this party was a little bigger and was some kind of a work related thing, lots of important people and plenty of flashy cars. Everything was going great and we were having a blast parking all these sweet cars. But once everyone was in and the event started, we just sat around. After a few hours, a secretary came out, gave us a few sandwiches and sodas and said they were at the halfway point. So, we figured that meant at least another three or four hours of just sitting around. We knew it was unlikely anyone would be leaving in the next hour for sure. So what happened next was actually my fault. I talked Eric into taking one of the cars out for a spin."

"He figured no one would be the wiser," Scott said.

"Seriously, I thought it was harmless, and would be a blast. Eric was nervous, but eventually gave in with the condition that he'd drive, and it would be Randy's car, the one he'd driven before, at the club. It's a fire engine red Lamborghini convertible and that thing hauls! We didn't go far with it, didn't want anyone to see us. Eric knew of a deserted service highway that was perfect. It had little traffic and a straightaway that went for several miles. We got it up over one hundred in seconds. It was like we were floating."

"But you got caught." Jake said.

"Yeah, we got busted. Randy was waiting in the lot for us. When Eric saw him there he slammed on the brakes, which sent a rock up from under the tires and smack into the middle of the window shield. It cracked it good; looked like a spider web almost."

"What did Randy do?" Jake had met the guy once through David, and that was enough. He didn't envy David for having to deal with him on a regular basis, no matter how big a client the guy was.

"His voice was real calm and scary-like, much quieter than normal and his face was beet red, looked like he wanted to explode. All he said was that he'd come out to tell us they were wrapping up sooner than expected. Then he said to park the car out back in the garage where no one could see it and get back to work. Once everyone was gone, we'd talk." Danny paused for a moment to take a sip of ginger ale, and then continued.

"We were dreading the end of the shift. We knew we'd probably have to pay for the damage and neither one of us had that kind of money. We figured he'd tell our parents too and then we'd really be in trouble. When he finally came out to see us, after all the guests were gone, he was totally worked up, his face even redder than before. It was like his anger was just building the whole time. He screamed at us, kind of crazy-like, called us all kinds of stupid, useless. Said there was no way we were getting paid and he made us hand over all our tips. We didn't mind, though, since we figured we owed him way more than that."

"Did he tell your parents?" Jake assumed that he must have.

"No, that kind of surprised us a little. He said we still owed him and he'd find a way for us to work it off and it wouldn't be as a valet."

"What did he have you do?" The more Jake heard about Randy the more he didn't care for the guy.

"We ran errands for him, spur-of-the-moment stuff; anything from delivering a package to washing his cars or picking up his dry-cleaning. He called us his 'bitches'. Eric asked him a few times how much longer it would be before we worked off the damage. He never gave him a real answer though, just said, 'you've got a ways to go.'

We were getting sick of it. He even had us shoveling shit. Every week, we had to clean out the horse stable. That was nasty. Eric finally told him we were done and he lost it. Said 'I could fucking kill you for what you did to my car.' Eric didn't back down though and Randy was still steaming as we pulled out of the driveway. That was the day before Eric went missing. I'm not saying there's a connection, but the guy is kind of whacked."

"Thanks, Danny. We'll have a chat with Randy and check things out."

Jake and Scott dropped Danny off at his house and decided to pay Randy a visit. David had once mentioned that Randy worked out of a home office, so they figured they might catch him at home. His house was what Jake often thought of as a McMansion, probably pushing ten thousand square feet, and looked like a massive box, three stories high, with a giant wrap-around farmer's porch and oversized glass windows throughout. It was a style that Jake had always found distasteful. The goal was clearly for show. Who needed a house that big? Especially when it was just the two of them living there.

They pulled down the driveway, which was long and winding and had a gorgeous view of the property, which was a three-acre lot, with plenty of trees and a manicured lawn. To the rear of the house was a stable that held several horses. David had also mentioned that Randy didn't ride, but his wife was an avid equestrian.

They parked and walked to the door and Randy's wife, Sharon answered. Her stomach was enormous. It looked as if she was ready to give birth any moment.

"Officers, how can I help you? Please come in." She opened the door wide and stepped back to let them pass through.

"Thank you. Is Randy in? We'd like to talk with him for a minute."

A confused look flashed across her face, but then she smiled and said, "Of course, I'll get him."

As she padded off to find her husband, Jake and Scott glanced around the room. They were in the main foyer, which opened into a kitchen nook with a cozy fireplace that was blasting out heat they could feel from where they were standing. Jake had expected a showier look, all high-end fancy furnishings, but what they could see of the kitchen area was more informal, even down to earth. Jake figured that must be Sharon's influence.

"How are you feeling?" he asked her as she returned with her husband in tow.

"Me? Oh, I'm fine. I just can't wait to get this baby out. It'll be any day now. My due date is tomorrow, but my doctor thinks I still have another week."

"You wanted to see me?" Randy's said in a clipped tone. He was clearly annoyed to be disturbed.

"Yes, we'd like to chat with you for a few minutes if that's okay?" Jake said.

"All right. I was in the middle of a project," he muttered.

"This won't take long."

"Why don't you sit in the breakfast room by the fire? Can I get anyone something to drink?"

"No thank you." Jake and Scott said at the same time.

They sat at a small round table by the fire and Randy looked impatient, waiting for them to begin.

"I understand that Eric Armstrong and Danny Wells did some work for you."

"If you could call it that," he said.

"Can you tell us how long they worked for you and what they did?"

"Not long, maybe a little over a month. I'd hired Eric because he treated my car with respect at the club when he was on valet duty. He and his friend, Danny, didn't do as good a job when he worked for me. They took my Lamborghini for a joyride and ruined it."

"They totaled the car?" Jake asked.

"Close enough. They hit a rock that shattered the windshield and damaged the underside of the car." Danny hadn't mentioned any damage besides the window.

"How bad was the damage to the underside?" he asked.

"It was nicked, but the whole thing will need to be painted and I had to replace the window shield. They were supposed to work off the damage, but they quit on me."

"That must have made you angry," Scott said.

"Hell, yeah. Kids these days have no work ethic, no sense of what things cost."

"Danny said you were furious, that you threatened to kill Eric."

Randy's jaw clenched and Jake could sense his anger building before he spoke. "That's ridiculous. I may have said something to that effect, but it was just talk—you know—things you say when you're pissed off."

"Right. Can you recall where you were the night Eric disappeared?"

"That's easy enough. There was an event at the club that night; both Sharon and I were there."

Jake and Scott exchanged glances and then Jake stood up.

"Okay, that's all we need. We'll be in touch if we have any further questions."

"I'm happy to help. It's a shame what happened to that kid." Randy's tone was more pleasant now and more relaxed now that he'd given them what seemed to be an ironclad alibi.

A few minutes later as they drove away from the house, Scott echoed what Jake was thinking.

"Too bad he seems to have a pretty good alibi, one that can easily be checked. I'd love to have him be our guy."

25

Lauren was having a great day. She'd had her yearly review that morning and had received nothing but 'exceeds expectations.'

"We're lucky to have you," Emily, the principal had said. "Please keep doing whatever you're doing. It works."

That had put her in a good mood for the entire day, which seemed to fly by. And she was looking forward to that evening and dinner with David. He'd called earlier and said Chuck and Katy had tickets they weren't able to use, as Katy was sick with a flu bug, would they be interested?

The tickets were for the musical Wicked, which was playing at the Opera House in Boston. Lauren had heard great things about Wicked and was looking forward to seeing a show at the Opera House, which was completely renovated and was supposed to be spectacular.

She and Amy finished up at about the same time and

walked out together. As soon as they stepped outside Lauren saw a lone minivan with KATV emblazoned on its side. The sight of even one van made her stomach sink.

"What do you suppose is going on?" Amy asked.

"I haven't the slightest." Lauren told herself to relax, that it was just one van and more than likely here for something student-related, and nothing to do with her.

They had to walk directly by the van, as it was parked front and center of the main school entrance and walkway. Lauren realized she was holding her breath a little as they got near. They were just about past the van and she was starting to relax a little when the side door flew open, and a smiley-faced pretty, young reporter with a blonde bob and pearls came running toward them.

"Are you Lauren Stanhope?" She asked.

Lauren nodded and braced herself.

"I'm Betty Cummings from WATZ. Miss Stanhope, is it true that you once confessed to murder?"

Lauren's jaw dropped. Whatever she expected, it wasn't this. She didn't think this was possible. She was a minor then and the court records were sealed. She felt a wave of anger wash over her and took a deep breath before answering. She knew she had to be very careful what she said now. If she just said 'no comment', she knew that most people would read that as being as good as guilty.

"I have never murdered anyone," Lauren said quietly and added, "and in the case you are referencing, that confession was tossed out of court."

That stopped the perkiness for a moment, but then Betty

bounced back and tried again, "But Lauren, you did confess to murder didn't you?"

Lauren responded to that by simply turning her back and walking away. Amy stuck close to her side until they were at their cars. Lauren knew she was dying to know what the reporter was talking about and since it was obviously going to be in the news anyway, she might as well fill her in on the whole sorry saga.

"Come over. We can talk over coffee and you can help me pick out what to wear tonight. I'll fill you in on my sordid past." She tried to joke a little about it, but Amy looked more worried than amused.

A half hour later, Lauren and Amy were sitting in the kitchen, and over coffee Lauren filled Amy in on what had happened so many years ago.

"You know, I vaguely remember hearing something about that, but it had all blown over by the time David and I moved here with our mother. I never realized Jake and Billy were involved. It makes sense now that Jake went into law enforcement. Funny that neither of them ever recognized you." She looked closely at Lauren. "Did you look very different then?"

"Well, obviously I was a lot younger." She said with a smile. "But I also wore glasses then and that can make a big difference in how people remember you; and my hair was darker. Plus, changing my name was the key—it took away any real connection. I get the occasional 'you look so familiar' from people, but until now, no one has connected the dots."

"Obviously David knows about this."

"Yes, I told him a little over a week ago, and he's been nothing but supportive."

Amy's eyebrows rose at that and she asked somewhat tentatively, "You only just told him this a week ago?"

Lauren picked up a hint of criticism in her tone and immediately felt defensive. "I never saw a need or a reason to mention it. I didn't do anything wrong, none of us did and that was all in the past. I didn't see the sense in dredging it up."

Amy weighed that for a moment. "I can see that. I can also imagine how surprised David must have been when you told him."

"Like I said, David has been very supportive. Are you done with your coffee?" Lauren jumped up and when Amy nodded yes, she picked up both mugs, rinsed them in the sink and then put them in the dishwasher. Amy wasn't done with the conversation though.

"Do Jake and Billy know who you are?" she asked.

"Jake does."

"And Billy doesn't?"

"No, I don't think so."

"I can't imagine this will be good for his business and David's business once word gets out," she said.

"Maybe I should have David talk to him, give him the heads up before this hits the papers, which will likely be tomorrow I imagine." She said and sighed.

"You might want to give him a call now," Amy suggested. "In case he tunes in to tonight's evening news."

"That's right. Thanks." Lauren glanced at the clock; it was

a little past 4:30 p.m. David would probably be taking off around five.

Amy got up and gave Lauren a hug. "I'll see you in the morning. In fact, if you want we can ride in together tomorrow."

Lauren felt her defensive mood slip away. Amy was still there for her and she had a feeling she would be grateful for that support tomorrow morning, when it was highly likely that there would be more than one minivan waiting for her.

26

David was ahead of schedule and planning to head out a little early, so he and Lauren could head into Boston with plenty of time to have dinner at Abe and Louie's, one of their favorite restaurants before the show. It was a few minutes past 4:30 and he was hoping to duck out by 4:45. But then the phone rang and it was Lauren, and after talking for a few minutes, he agreed that he needed to sit down with Billy and give him a heads up.

"Got a minute?" Billy was just setting his phone down as David popped his head in the door.

"Sure, come on in. What's up?" David closed the door behind him and sat in a comfortable leather chair facing Billy.

"We need to talk."

"You sound serious. Is something wrong? Is it your grandfather?" Billy looked worried. His phone rang and he buzzed Trudy at the front desk to tell her to hold his calls—that he and David were in a meeting.

"No, Gramps is good. It's Lauren. Actually, it's not just Lauren; it's also you and Jake and the case you guys were part of years ago with the false confessions. A reporter caught wind of it and confronted Lauren as she was leaving school today. Looks like it's going to be on the news tonight and likely will hit the papers tomorrow."

"What does Lauren have to do with that old case?"

"Remember Melissa Hopkins?"

"Yeah, she was the girl that confessed with us."

"That's Lauren." He explained about the move out west and the name change.

"That's pretty crazy. Funny that she came back here after all these years."

"She always considered Waverly home, and that old case buried in the past. Thought it would be a non-issue."

"Probably would have been." Billy frowned and tapped his pen a few times against his notebook.

"You know, those records were supposed to be sealed. We were all minors," he said thoughtfully.

"That's what I thought at first too, but then I realized it made the news back then because it was so unusual for three confessions to be tossed out and deemed coerced. That case and a few others set a new precedent for how interrogations could be conducted."

"That's right," Billy agreed then added, "This might not be so good for business."

"I know. That's why I wanted to give you a heads up before you were blind-sided by the news."

"Any suggestions for how we handle this? The media is bound to come calling."

"I'm thinking that the less said the better. We don't want to feed this story."

"Right. So maybe just a simple statement reiterating that we were all found innocent and that the confessions were considered forced."

"And that we support Lauren completely."

"Of course. We'll get through this," Billy said confidently. Billy faced everything with confidence, an innate sureness that everything would go his way. And it usually did. David hoped that would be the case here as well.

27

So how did Billy take it?" Lauren asked as soon as David got home. She was all dressed and ready to go. David didn't need to change so he just dropped off his briefcase and filled her in on the conversation as they walked to the car and then started driving in to Boston.

"Overall, it went about as well as could be expected. Billy doesn't get all hung up about the past. His main concern is handling this well so that it doesn't hurt the business."

"I don't blame him. And it's not just his business, it's yours, too," Lauren reminded him.

"I'm not worried about myself. We'll get through this. Let's just relax and enjoy tonight."

And they did. Abe and Louis' was fantastic as usual. They both ordered steaks and Lauren saved room for dessert, a decadent, six-layer chocolate cake. The first time they'd come here, she'd watched half a dozen of the cakes go by while they were eating and couldn't wait to try a piece herself. It was probably the best chocolate cake she'd ever had, rich and moist and exceeding her expectations completely. Now it was a given that dinner at Abe and Louis' meant chocolate cake.

After dinner, they walked over to the Opera House to see the show, which was spectacular, and the theatre was packed to capacity. The theatre itself was gorgeous. The renovations had kept the old feel of the intricate architecture with all the sculpted ceiling moldings and lush colors, and yet had a slightly modern feel as well, with larger seats and a bit of an art deco feeling with black and white marble floors. The mood was festive; there were people drinking champagne and dressed to the nines.

As they were exiting the building, Lauren tensed up immediately when she saw a row of media vans and a throng of paparazzi on the sidewalk.

"What the..." David began, and grabbed Lauren's hand as they made their way through the crowds and toward the media, which could not be avoided. But, they let them pass right by without even a second glance and Lauren breathed a sigh of relief. It wouldn't have made sense for that much media to be there for her, especially here in Boston, but it was still unsettling.

They both glanced back to see who was the target, and a moment later the actor Matt Damon and his lovely wife, Louisa, walked out followed by Jake Nicholson and an elegantly dressed woman. Lauren recalled reading something in the Herald about a new movie filming around Boston starring Matt Damon and Jake Nicholson. Both stars were popular with the media and the public, and watching how they interacted with everyone, she could understand why.

The two stars were gracious, taking turns answering questions from the media, shaking hands and signing autographs for fans. They never stopped smiling. David and Lauren kept walking and when they reached their car, in a lot a few blocks down, she glanced back at the theatre again and saw the two stars were still there, surrounded by fans and media. She shuddered as she hopped into the car and buckled her seatbelt.

"I really sympathize for them," she said.

"Who? Damon and Nicholson. You feel sorry for them? They're used to it. It's a small price to pay for the many millions they both make."

"I suppose. They have no privacy though. People, especially the media, follow them everywhere. I'd hate that."

"It's not the same," David said.

"I'd just be happy if I never see another media van again."

"This will blow over soon. As soon as they catch whoever did this to Eric, their focus will shift. I think the worst of it is past."

"I hope you're right." Lauren still had an uneasy sense that some kind of trouble was still simmering. She tried to shake the feeling off, but couldn't get rid of it completely.

They got home a little before midnight, but Lauren had set the DVR to record the eleven o'clock news. She and David undressed, then climbed into bed and turned on the news. They fast-forwarded until they saw Jake's face and stopped to listen. Barbie Montgomery, one of the youngest and blondest of the perky reporters was in the field, interviewing Jake just outside the station.

"So, does this concern you that your only real suspect in this case has a history of murder?" she asked sweetly, batting her suspiciously long eyelashes and smiling non-stop.

"First of all, Lauren is not a suspect and never has been. Second of all, there is no history of murder. Lauren and two others, me included I might add, were coerced into giving false confessions to a murder over twenty years ago. Those confessions were garbage and were rightly tossed out. This information is meaningless. There's no story here." He looked furious and Lauren loved him for it. Jake was a great friend.

"Okay, well thank you for that. Live from Waverly, Mass., this is Barbie Montgomery. We're going back to Bill in the studio now. Bill, what do you think of this?"

The camera flashed to anchorman, Bill Pendleton, and his sidekick, Jenna Carlson. Bill was in his mid-fifties, a seasoned pro who had been with the station for over twenty years. Jenna, on the other hand, was in her late twenties and preppy-pretty, with long shiny blonde hair, parted neatly in the middle and falling just past her shoulders. She wore fashionable black glasses that were supposed to make her look smarter, but as soon as she opened her mouth and spoke in that high, breathy, little-girl voice, the illusion was immediately shattered.

"It certainly makes you wonder," he said slowly, and then Jenna piped in, "Where there's smoke there's fire, right?"

"Speaking of fire," Bill began, "we're going live to Jose in Mattapan where a three alarm fire is raging."

David clicked off the TV and turned to Lauren, "Jake was good, and credible. Hopefully, people won't put much stock in this latest 'revelation.'"

28

Amy picked Lauren up the next morning and when they pulled into the school parking lot, Lauren braced herself for an onslaught of hungry media. But, much to her surprise and relief, there wasn't a single van waiting.

"Maybe they got all they needed on this, or realized that Jake was right and there's no story here," Amy said.

"Thank god," Lauren said as she got out of the car and grabbed her tote bag and coffee. Maybe Jake and David were right and people were smart enough to realize this really was a non-issue.

After school, Amy and Lauren went over to Nellie's to pick up their dresses. Lauren was in a fabulous mood. It seemed like the media insanity might be over and now she could concentrate on the wedding, which was a week and a half away.

Plus, it was snowing again, big fat flakes slowly floating

down. The snow had started a few hours ago and was expected to keep on through the night. It didn't look like much of a storm now, but the winds and intensity were supposed to pick up overnight. The kids in her last period class were all excited, and wishing verbally for a snow day tomorrow. Lauren had to admit the idea appealed to her as well. She wouldn't mind a day off to curl up and watch old movies while the snow swirled outside.

When they arrived at Nellie's place, Lauren saw that she had the house decorated for Christmas. Delicate strings of white lights blinked merrily along the many well-groomed hedges, all along the Gingerbread trimming, and around the railing of the farmer's porch. The front door held a shiny silver wreath of jingle bells tied with a shimmery purple ribbon. Lauren recognized the wreath came from the Pottery Barn and she had the same one at home.

The door opened before they had a chance to knock. Nellie had been keeping an eye out for them.

"Come in, come in. This weather is terrible!"

They entered the front hall foyer and per Nellie's instructions took off their shoes and then followed her down the hall to the sewing room.

"Now try these on again real quick. Make sure they both fit the way you like. Lauren, you first." She carefully handed Lauren the wedding dress and held the curtain of the dressing room back so she could enter. Lauren held her breath as she slipped on the dress, hoping that it wouldn't be too tight since that would be hard to fix with so little time before the wedding. But she relaxed as she saw the dress fit perfectly with no tight spots anywhere. She stepped out of the dressing room for Amy and Nellie to see. Nellie took a step back and peered intensely at the dress from every angle, asking Lauren to do a slow turnaround.

"You look beautiful!" Amy said.

"The fit is good," Nellie said and seemed satisfied with her work.

"It's absolutely perfect! Thank you so much." Amy was next and her dress was also a success. When they were both in their regular clothes again, Nellie zipped each dress into a tight, protective cover and then insisted that they both join her for a hot chocolate in the study.

"You don't have to ask me twice," Lauren said. "Amy, what about you?"

"Of course." Nellie led them into her small study, which was at the front corner of the house overlooking the Farmer's porch and Main St.

"Thanks," Lauren said when Nellie returned a moment later with two steaming mugs of hot chocolate with mini-marshmallows bobbing on top. "You have a great view here."

"This is my favorite room," Nellie said proudly as she settled into a padded rocker that faced the window. "I sit here most afternoons with my knitting. I play a little jazz or big band music and watch all the activity out front, the kids coming home from school, trolley's going by, and people out walking their dogs."

"That sounds relaxing," Amy said before taking a tentative sip of the very hot chocolate.

"I don't miss much," Nellie added. "If something happens in this neighborhood, I know about it. Just before you got here for example, I saw at least a half- dozen of those media vans come bombing down the road. Going way too fast if you ask me. Don't know where they were going, but they were in a real hurry to get there."

Lauren and Amy exchanged glances. "We should probably get going," Amy said.

"Wait a minute. Let me turn on the police scanner, see what's going on. It might be a bad accident or something. You don't want to get stuck in traffic." Nellie switched on the ancient police scanner that sat on a little side table, in easy reach of her rocking chair. No wonder she didn't miss much. The radio crackled, then the static eased out, and a moment later, they could hear voices talking.

"The old Graybar building finally went. Fell right off the cliff and into the ocean. On my way now."

"Well, isn't that something." Nellie said. "That old building has been teetering for years. It was the only one left." Erosion was a big problem in some parts of Waverly. The Graybar building was once a stately home and turned into a bed and breakfast years ago, but for the past ten years had sat empty and waiting for a storm strong enough to shake it loose.

That stretch of cliff had been hit especially hard over the years and one-by-one each home had toppled into the sea, with some of the worst Nor'easters taking more than one at a time. Graybar was the only one left and they were not allowed to build in that area.

"The waves out there must be ferocious," Lauren said. Whenever there was a particularly bad storm, the media tended to flock to Waverly for storm coverage of giant waves crashing over the rocks and onto the streets.

"The eleven o'clock news will be exciting tonight," Nellie said. "Still, it's a shame to see it happen."

29

I think we need to take a closer look at Randy," Jake said. The lights flickered for a moment in the office as the snowstorm raged outside. It was nearly five o'clock and the winds had really kicked in out there. Five officers were sitting in Jake's office reviewing their notes on the Eric Armstrong case. They were still waiting for the DNA results to come back from the lab in Boston.

"I don't like the guy much either," Scott said, "but he does have an alibi."

"Yeah, but it's his wife. I'm not sure how much stock I'd put in that," Chris the younger officer said.

"I'm inclined to agree with Chris," Jake said "And so far, he's the only one who has any kind of motive."

"I don't know if I'd agree with that," Scott said. "He has a temper and he was annoyed with the kid, but a reason to kill? Not so sure about that."

"He's a hot-head though," Chris said. "He could have just snapped."

"We still need to look more closely at Lauren. Jake I know you're friends with her, but it seems to me like she might have a pretty good motive here. If she was fooling around with the kid, maybe she tried to end it and he got all upset and threatened to go public. She stood to lose her job and her fiancé."

"That's nothing but speculation," Jake said dismissively. "There's no evidence that there was any kind of inappropriate relationship between the two of them. So, no relationship means no motive."

"There were people who thought something was going on. His friends wondered, said he was spending a lot of time outside of class with his hot English teacher. And there was his online journal talking about the 'mad crush' and hot 'older woman.'"

"Lauren admitted to spending time after class with Eric, but she was counseling him, trying to help him do better. He may have had a crush on her. In fact, it wouldn't surprise me a bit. But it doesn't mean it was mutual."

"I wonder about his parents." Tim, another of the senior officers, spoke up. "The father was known to be a drinker and to have an ugly temper. In her statement, Lauren said Eric talked about trouble at home. Maybe he's the one that snapped."

"He has an alibi too." Jake said.

"Right, his wife. Did you notice how timid she becomes whenever he's around? I think she'd say whatever he told her to say."

Jake rubbed his temple, willing away the beginnings of a stress headache.

"All right, let's regroup tomorrow, dig deeper into all of this and see what emerges. Drive safely out there everyone, it's looking nasty."

30

Lauren slept in the next day and stretched lazily in her bed. It was still snowing heavily outside and she could see several sharp icicles hanging just outside the bedroom window. The call from school went out last night—there would be no classes today. Lauren suspected she was as excited by that news as her students were.

She flipped on the TV and landed on the local station where they were showing coverage of the Graybar house. The waves hitting the cliff were massive, reminding her of the giant surf you see in Hawaii and rarely saw in the northeast, except for particularly bad storms like this. The media got there too late to capture the house falling into the ocean, but a few teenagers were there and shot the footage on their own camcorders.

The video was obviously amateurish, wobbly and blurry in parts, but the overall image of the house tumbling into the sea was spellbinding and surreal. It looked more like a Hollywood special effect than a real event. The rest of the news was tame in comparison, and after a few minutes, Lauren switched off the TV and rolled out of bed.

She stayed in her pajamas most of the day, lounging on the sofa downstairs, wrapped in a soft fleece throw and watching old movies. Every now and then she got up to grab a snack or a bowl of soup. By mid-afternoon, she was movied-out, jumped in the shower and then got to work in the kitchen.

She was going to make braised short ribs and had taken the meat out of the freezer first thing in the morning to defrost. The snow was still coming down hard outside and she was glad that David's car had four-wheel drive and that he didn't have far to go. His office was just a few miles down the road. He'd called earlier to say they were going to wrap up around 4:00 so people could get home before dark and before the roads got too icy.

Lauren went to work chopping the vegetables to add to the braise. She liked to have all her ingredients ready and prepped in small bowls before she started cooking. Short ribs were one of her favorite things to make, and were the ideal comfort food in weather like this. The final dish would be similar to a rich stew, with a silky sauce of reduced wine, beef broth and aromatics over meat that was fall-off-the-bone tender from slow cooking for several hours.

Once the onions, carrots and celery were finely chopped and in their respective bowls, Lauren pulled out her giant sauté pan—the one that was wide and about five inches deep— and set it on her largest burner. Everything would happen in that pan. First, she added a little olive oil and heated it until it started to crackle, then she browned the short ribs in batches until they were all deep brown and caramelized on the outside. She then set the meat aside on a platter, dumped the vegetables into the pan and stirred them as they cooked to release the brown bits that were stuck on the bottom.

These would contribute great flavor to the sauce. Once the vegetables were soft and slightly brown, she added a full bottle of full-bodied red wine and let it reduce down to about a cup of liquid, which would intensify the flavor for the braising liquid. She added a cup and one-half of tawny port and the same amount of beef broth, then put the short ribs in, covered the pan and set it in the oven to simmer at 325° for three hours.

While the meat was simmering away in the oven, Lauren curled up on the sofa with the latest Jodi Picoult novel. By a quarter to five, when David came walking through the door, the house smelled amazing and her stomach rumbled a little in anticipation. David shook off the snow from his jacket, took it off and stepped out of his boots.

"I think I've died and gone to heaven," he said. "Would you believe I left the office at 4:00 sharp? I've been sitting in gridlock traffic for the past forty-five minutes. The plows can barely keep up with it." His ride home normally took, at the most, five minutes.

"This should be just about done. I'm going to pull it out of the oven and let it rest for a few minutes. Do you want a glass of wine first?"

"That sounds great. I'm going to run upstairs and change into some sweats. Be down in a minute." While he was upstairs, Lauren opened a new bottle of wine, the same kind she'd used in the braise, poured two glasses and set them down on the coffee table by the sofa she'd been curled up on. She hit the switch on the gas fireplace and the flames roared high enough that she could feel the heat. David joined her a few minutes later and settled next to her on the sofa with his feet up on the coffee table.

"So how was your day?" Lauren asked as she took a sip of the wine.

"Okay. Chuck was in a mood though. Sounds like he and Katy are going through a rough patch. Whenever they don't get along, he's a bear to be around."

"That's too bad. They haven't been married long to be having difficulties I wouldn't think."

"Well, they actually dated for years, but only lived together for the past year, once they got married. I get the sense from a few comments he's made that it's been a bit of an adjustment for both of them. Chuck's always been a loner of sorts. I think he misses having his own space."

"This weather probably doesn't help much," Lauren said. "They'll really get on each other's nerves if this storm keeps up and they have to stay inside for a few days."

"He was still there when I left, and didn't look like he was planning on going anywhere for a while." Chuck lived close by work too, so he could always walk home if need be.

"Have you heard from any clients since the news piece aired, are they upset?" Lauren was concerned that Billy's fears could come true and that they'd lose clients.

"Surprisingly, no. We've had a few clients call, but only to voice their support and contempt for the media."

"That's reassuring. I think people are smart enough to see through the garbage the media tries to serve up."

"For the most part, yes. But not always."

"Are you hungry? The short ribs are ready if you are."

"I'm starving and they smell incredible."

Lauren had opened a container of Country Crock mashed potatoes a half-hour earlier and they were keeping warm in a big saucepan. She put a generous mound of the potatoes in two large bowls and then spooned the meaty short ribs and plenty of sauce over the top. David brought their glasses of wine to the dining room table and Lauren had just taken her first bite when the phone rang. David answered and then handed the phone to her, "It's Jake, he said he needs to talk to you. It sounds important."

31

Jake had been sitting in his office, staring at his computer screen for a good thirty minutes before picking up the phone. The DNA lab results had come in and as expected, they confirmed that the blood on the golf club belonged to Eric Armstrong. They had a match on the fingerprints too and those results were not at all expected.

Jake was having a difficult time coming to terms with the fact that the prints on the golf club were a perfect match to Lauren Stanhope. What he should do is go right over, arrest Lauren, have her spend the weekend in jail and then go to court on Monday to see about bail.

But, no one else had access to the fingerprint report in his office, so he could delay acting on this for a few days. He needed to have a talk with Lauren though, to see what, if anything, she had to say that could shed light on how one of her clubs ended up as a murder weapon. And he needed to warn her things were likely to get very ugly once the media caught wind of this, which they would as soon as she was arrested.

If he did it now, the media would go crazy with the story all weekend, whereas if he could hold off until Monday and she could be granted bail quickly, they could maybe keep the media at bay somewhat, though Jake had his doubts about that too.

"Lauren, it's Jake. Are you and David in for the night?"

"Yes, what's up?"

"I'm done for the day and need to talk to you in person. I'm on my way." He hung up before she had a chance to respond, so Lauren clicked her phone off as well and turned to David who was looking at her for an explanation.

"Jake is coming over to talk to me. But I have no idea why."

They returned to their meal and ate in silence, all the enjoyment gone. Forty-five minutes later, they were done eating, dishes were in the dishwasher, and Lauren had packed the rest of the short ribs into a large glass bowl for storage in the refrigerator.

She'd just topped off both of their wine glasses and they were back on the sofa, flipping channels on the TV, but not really paying attention. Instead, they were both anxious about Jake's visit. Finally, the knock came on the door and David jumped up to let Jake in.

"Would you like a glass of wine or a beer?"

He declined the offer for a drink and sat in the overstuffed leather chair across from where they were both sitting on the sofa. "I still need to get home from here and unfortunately this isn't a social call. This isn't easy for me, so I'm just going to come out with it."

He paused and then looked directly at Lauren, "The results came back from the golf club we found and thought might be the murder weapon in the Eric Armstrong case. The DNA is Eric's. We also got a match on the fingerprints. Lauren, they're yours. Do you have any idea why that would be?"

"My golf club killed Eric Armstrong?" Lauren couldn't believe it.

"When was the last time you played golf?" Jake asked.

"Several weeks ago, before Eric went missing. Jake you don't think I did this? What is going on here?" Fear swept through her.

Jake sighed deeply. "It doesn't matter what I think. Where do you keep your clubs?"

"In the trunk of my car."

"Can we go take a look?"

"Sure, we can go right through the kitchen to the garage." Lauren's voice was shaking as she spoke and David looked at both of them in disbelief.

"Jake, this is ridiculous. What are you doing?" He jumped up from the sofa and started to pace.

"My job. I don't have a choice." Jake's jaw was clenched and as bewildered as she felt, Lauren felt a pang of sympathy for him as well. He didn't look at all happy to be here, doing this to his friends.

"Are you going to arrest me?" she asked; it all felt so surreal.

"Yes, I'll have to," he said, "but I can do it first thing Monday, that way you won't have to spend the weekend in jail. Hopefully, they'll grant you bail and you'll be out the same day."

"Well, that's something." David said in a sullen tone.

Lauren shuddered at the thought of spending even one night in jail, but as upset as she was she realized the enormous favor that Jake was doing her. "Jake, thank you. This doesn't make any sense at all."

She opened the trunk of her car and pulled out her set of clubs. They were all there, all except one, her three-wood.

"Did you know you were missing a club?" Jake asked.

"Yes, I lost it on the course last time I played. Accidentally set it down. I called right away to let the club know if someone found it and brought it in to call me. Eric actually called me the next day. It was returned during his shift. He said he'd put a tag on it and keep it under the counter and I could just pick it up the next time I came in. I was supposed to play a few days later, but that got canceled at the last minute and I haven't been back since."

"Was there anyone else's prints on the club?" David asked.

"Yes, there would have to be right?" Lauren said excitedly.

"There were several sets of prints, Lauren's, Eric's and several unidentified ones."

"Well that's good right? If there were other prints on the club then you can't assume that Lauren did anything. Especially if her club was missing."

"That will definitely work in her favor," Jake agreed. "It will be difficult to prove guilt beyond a reasonable doubt with additional prints on the club raising the possibility that someone else could have done this. We'll have to request prints from all club members and staff."

"So, you won't have to arrest Lauren then?" David said with relief.

"No, I'll still have to arrest her. It's all part of the process. Do you want these clubs back in your trunk?"

"I'll keep them here. I think my golfing days are over for this year."

"Right, well I'm sure I don't need to tell you both to keep this to yourselves over the weekend?"

"Jake, should I just come in to see you first thing on Monday?" Lauren asked.

"Yes, I'll try to make it as painless as possible. But it's still going to be rough going for a while."

Lauren thought that was likely an understatement. Her stomach was already in knots just thinking about what the media would do with this.

"Okay, I'm going to run. Lauren, the earlier the better on Monday. The sooner we get you in, the sooner, you'll be home." He stepped out into the storm and David shut the door tightly behind him.

"Lauren, this is insane." David reached for his glass of wine and took a huge sip. Lauren felt her eyes well up and simply said, "I know." She picked up her wine and settled back onto the sofa and David joined her.

"What are we going to do? I didn't do anything, you know that, right?" The tears started to fall and she blotted at her eyes with the back of her hand. David grabbed her other hand and squeezed it tight.

"Of course. I know you. I love you. We will get through

this. I'll talk to Gramps in the morning. He'll have an idea on who we should call for an attorney."

"An attorney." Lauren hadn't even thought of that, but of course, she had to have an attorney. She felt a bit of deja vu coming over her. This had the same surreal feeling as what she'd gone through so many years ago. It was like she was being pulled under. She wrapped the soft fleece throw tightly around her and felt hot tears spill over.

"You should leave a message now for the school. Tell them you won't be in on Monday, that you're taking a personal day."

Lauren sniffled and grabbed a tissue. "I suppose I should. David, what if people don't believe me? Could I actually be found guilty for something I didn't do? For murder?" Were her fingerprints on what was evidently the murder weapon enough? And then an even worse thought, "What if I have to go to jail?"

"We are not going to let that happen." David's voice was confident and firm and Lauren wanted to believe him. But her confidence was slipping away.

32

Lauren barely slept all weekend. She and David were like a couple of robots, going through the motions and watching the clock tick the minutes and hours away. She'd done as David had suggested, left a message at school saying she'd be out on Monday and David had done the same at work. He insisted on going with her on Monday, driving her in and being there for support. Although Jake had given them a big break by holding the arrest off until Monday, they knew that was all he could do. They were both worried sick, because without another real suspect, Lauren was it, and a murder weapon with her prints on it was going to make up a lot of people's minds.

They arrived just before 7:30 on Monday morning and met their attorney in the parking lot. His name was Evan McSweeney and Lauren liked him instantly. Evan was in his late forties, had thick black hair with a sprinkling of gray. David's grandfather said Evan was the best.

She'd had a quick phone call with him over the weekend and brought him up to speed on everything. He told her not to worry and to be as cooperative as possible and that he'd be right there with her. They walked in together and David asked for Jake. He came right out and led them into his office, filled out paperwork and asked a series of questions, all of which Lauren had already been asked and answered previously.

She did it again though, anxious to get through the day somehow. Once Jake had everything he needed, he led them into a waiting area. The next step would be to go before the judge and arrange for bail. Evan didn't anticipate they'd have any resistance there.

"You don't have any kind of history to speak of, and are getting married in less than a week. It's a pretty good bet that you're not a flight risk."

"Have to admit it's a little tempting," Lauren said wistfully.

"Don't even joke about something like that," David said.

"If I don't laugh about this, I could go crazy," Lauren said. "It's going to get really bad isn't it?" she asked Evan and he didn't hesitate in his answer.

"Yes, it will likely get ugly once the media catches wind of this, and it won't take them long." David reached over and squeezed her hand and she gave him a small smile even though she really felt like crying.

"You may have to take a leave of absence from work,"

Evan added. "I wouldn't be at all surprised if they suggest that to you. They'll want to appease the parents."

"But that's so unfair!" David said. It hadn't even crossed Lauren's mind that the school could ask her to do that.

"It's not like I'd have a choice is it? I suppose I wouldn't really blame the parents."

David started to object but Lauren cut him off, "David think about it, if you had kids and a teacher was accused of something like this, and there was hard evidence; well, it looks pretty damning. I don't think I'd be comfortable with that teacher staying on either."

"It might actually be easier for you in a way. You know the media will be relentless, camping outside school and so on. If you're home, they will have to keep their distance."

A few minutes later, Lauren's name was called and she and Evan went before the judge. "I've reviewed your record and it's troubling, but there is no prior history here and based on that I'm allowing bail to be set at $5,000."

Evan helped them make arrangements to pay the bail and a court date was set for three weeks out for the arraignment.

"So that's it? I just go home now?" Lauren asked. It was all so overwhelming and still so early in the day, not even 1:00 p.m. yet.

"That's it. You might want to get some lunch, but yes, now we wait." Evan waved goodbye as he got into his silver Mercedes sedan and pulled out of the lot. Lauren and David just stood there, watching Evan drive away and then looked at each other.

"I don't want to go home yet, do you?" David asked. "Let's

go grab some lunch, pretend it's just a day off, get our minds off things for a little while."

"All right," Lauren agreed. She realized that she wasn't ready to go home yet either.

When they arrived home after having a couple of beers and turkey club sandwiches at the pub, Lauren felt full and a little less stressed. She actually felt like curling up and taking a nap. Turkey always seemed to have that effect on her. She fought the urge though, because she knew if she napped now she'd never get to sleep later. David disappeared into the den to check his e-mail and do a little work and Lauren decided to keep busy doing projects around the house.

She had plenty of laundry that needed to be done and started by stripping the beds and throwing in a load of sheets and dirty towels. If she kept busy, maybe her mind would quiet down. She decided to make chicken soup. Mindlessly she chopped the vegetables she'd need for the soup—carrots, onions and celery. She threw them into a big pot along with a chicken she'd picked up over the weekend. She added water and a bay leaf and turned the heat on high, then once it reached a boil, she turned it down to simmer for a few hours.

Even though they were both full from lunch, she knew they'd want something light later. Around four in the afternoon,, the phone started to ring and she let the machine pick up. Word was out—it was one of the local newspapers calling. She knew the others would be close behind and sure enough, at least a dozen other calls came in over the next few hours.

Lauren let them all go to voicemail. One of the reporters, a Barbie something, actually called three times.

Lauren listened to each message once and then deleted it. She found plenty of other things to do—magazines that had piled up and needed to be tossed, bills that had to be paid— and before she knew it, fresh sheets were on the bed, towels folded and put away and it was nearly time to eat again.

She and David sat in front of the TV with steaming bowls of soup on the coffee table and waited for the news to come on. When they said the name Barbie Montgomery, Lauren tensed.

"Thanks Bob, this is Barbie Montgomery, here in Waverly where we're following a breaking news story. Formerly a person of interest, teacher Lauren Stanhope, is now officially a suspect. She was arrested early this morning for the murder of Eric Armstrong, the student who some say she was allegedly having an affair with."

"How can she say that?" Lauren was outraged.

"Well, she's not saying it's factual, just that others are saying it might be so. It's a pretty slippery slope," he agreed.

"Eric Armstrong was killed with one of Lauren Stanhope's golf clubs, her three-wood and her fingerprints were confirmed as a match." Lauren thought that Barbie looked much too excited about this story.

"She's annoyingly perky," she said.

"They all are," David agreed.

"She's the worst though. She left me three messages. As if I would actually call her back."

"I'm sure you'll see her bright shiny face first thing in the morning." David teased.

"Ugh, maybe I'll take another personal day tomorrow." Lauren was dreading her first day back at school.

"I don't blame you, but you may want to just get it over with. It'll seem like you're hiding out if you stay away."

"You're right. I know that. I have to admit, I'm a little terrified."

"You can do it. I'll call Amy for you, fill her in on what's going on and I'm sure she'll offer to drive you in."

"Thanks, I'd appreciate that." She'd thought of calling Amy earlier, but was putting it off. She knew Amy would support her, but how exactly does someone say, "Oh, by the way, I was arrested this morning for murder?"

33

Amy beeped the horn the next morning at a quarter past
seven and Lauren peeked out the kitchen window. It
was already starting. Four media vans were parked outside
her condo and she'd have to walk directly in front of one of
them to get to Amy's car. She pulled her jacket tightly around
her and stepped outside, locking the front door behind her.
She walked quickly toward Amy's car and didn't make eye
contact with any of the vans. Still she heard a door open and
the tap-tap of high heels hitting the concrete, and then that
annoyingly perky high-pitched voice.

"Lauren, Barbie Montgomery here from WATV, can we
have a minute? Will you please talk to us Lauren?" But Lauren wouldn't even look up. She brushed by the reporter and
her cameraman and caught a glimpse of fluffy blond hair out
of the corner of her eye. Barbie was certainly persistent.

She reached the passenger side door of Amy's Ford Taurus, jumped in and locked the door.

"Thank you so much for driving me in today."

"David called me last night. I could hardly say no." But her tone was a little frosty and Lauren glanced at her with concern.

"Did he explain what happened?"

"Sort of. He said you were arrested. For murder, and that your fingerprints were on the murder weapon. It's a lot to digest."

"I didn't do anything!"

"I know. I want to believe that. I do. It's just that I don't understand why your golf club was used as a murder weapon."

"I don't know either. I'm just sick about this."

Amy's voice softened a little. "The thing that really worries me is that if they're going to be going after you this way, with an arrest, will they still put much effort into finding out who really did this? If they can find the real killer it will make all of this go away for you."

"I know. It's all I can think about, and according to what Jake has told us, they don't have any other real leads. It's frightening."

Amy pulled into the school parking lot and Lauren's stomach immediately clenched as she saw the parade of media waiting at the front entrance. At least a dozen vans and even more reporters and photographers lined the walkway. They all screamed out to her as she and Amy hurried inside. She ignored them all, but knew they wouldn't go away so easily, that they'd still be there when school let out.

Lauren went right to her office and turned on her computer. As it was booting up and she took her first sip of coffee, Emily, the school principal walked in and shut the door behind her.

"Lauren, you know I have the highest regard for you, both as a person and as a teacher," she began. Lauren nodded and waited for her to continue. She got to the point quickly.

"I've already arranged for a substitute teacher to take over your classes as of today. I think it's for the best, for your students and for you, if you take a leave of absence until this all blows over.

"David thought you might suggest that," Lauren said. "I agree. I'm sure the parents will be more comfortable, at least until this is resolved and I'm cleared.

"I look forward to that," Emily said kindly. "If you like, I can call a cab for you and have it meet you out back by the cafeteria loading zone, so the media won't see you."

"Thank you, I'd appreciate it." Lauren found herself fighting back tears as she gathered her things and said a quick goodbye to Amy. As she stood waiting for her cab in the shivering cold of the cafeteria's loading zone, it hit her hard that her life as she knew it was never going to be the same.

34

Barbie Montgomery sat in the passenger side of the van, sipping coffee and shivering with a mixture of excitement. She was thrilled to be right in the thick of this story and her boss had already given her kudos for breaking the former false confession angle. Now that there was a confirmed murder weapon with Lauren's prints on it, they really had a story. Open and shut as far as Barbie was concerned. No way Lauren didn't do this.

Barbie wondered why she'd been so foolish though to throw everything away. She had to know she'd get caught... and what about her wedding? She was due to marry someone in less than a week who, from all accounts, was a really great guy. And the student, Barbie had to admit that part of the story was a little hard to follow.

Unless the relationship with the boyfriend wasn't as solid as it appeared. Barbie knew all too well how deceiving appearances of the happy family could be. Plus the boy was an older-looking sixteen, and from the photos she'd seen, he was quite handsome. Still, that part of the story troubled her. Maybe this wasn't a totally open and shut case. Although, prints found on a murder weapon was pretty damning evidence.

"You want one?" Victor, her cameraman, was sitting next to her in the driver's seat munching on a glazed donut. There were two more in a crumpled bag by his side and they smelled heavenly. Barbie's stomach rumbled in appreciation. But having a donut was not an option. She struggled enough to maintain her weight as it was. The rumors about the camera adding ten to fifteen pounds? Totally true. She fished a chocolate flavored protein bar out of her tote bag instead and took a bite.

They were one of at least a dozen news organizations lobbying for position outside the school, all of them hoping for a photo opportunity or even a comment or two from Lauren. Barbie and Vic had been there for several hours already. It paid to be the first on scene. There was a strategy to where you parked. You wanted to size up the area and make sure your target had no choice but to walk by you. By the time she finished her protein bar though, Barbie had a new plan.

"Vic, let's get out of here. I want to position ourselves right in front of Lauren's condo."

"But we have the best spot here, we'll lose it."

But Barbie had been thinking, trying to imagine what must be happening inside the school and she realized it wasn't likely that Lauren was really going work today as if nothing had happened. The principal and many of the student's parents weren't likely to allow that.

"I'll bet you a dollar she's out of there within the hour. And I don't see her coming out our way. She got a ride in with a friend remember? Someone is coming to get her, whether it's a friend or a cab and she's going to sneak out another entrance. That's what I'd do anyway."

"All right, let's go." Victor fired up the engine and they eased out of their spot. Barbie looked back, and before they were out of the lot another van had claimed their spot.

"If we hurry, we might be able to beat her home," Barbie said.

Ten minutes later they were pulling down the street to Lauren's condo and parked right in front of her walkway so that she had to walk by them to get to her front door. Barbie was keyed up. She had a feeling they wouldn't be waiting long. Maybe, since it was just one van, Lauren wouldn't be as intimidated and might actually acknowledge them. She'd kill for an interview or even a comment or two, but knew that might be asking for too much. No doubt, she was lawyered up now and had been instructed to say nothing, especially to the media.

They didn't have to wait long. Barbie snapped to attention when she saw a yellow taxicab coming towards them. The car pulled up behind their van and it was Lauren. Barbie and Victor flew out of the van and waited for her to approach them.

"Lauren, Barbie Montgomery from WATV. Could we have a word?" Lauren stared at them in disbelief, dismayed that they were there. Obviously, she thought everyone would still be at the school. She was clearly stressed and looked like she'd barely slept. She put her head down and started walking quickly toward the door.

"Lauren, is there a connection between Eric's death and the one you confessed to twenty years ago?" That stopped her in her tracks.

"No, of course not!" she said and then immediately a look of horror came over her face. It was clear she'd been instructed to say nothing.

Barbie and Victor moved closer.

"So, are you admitting to this murder as well?" Barbie pressed. But Lauren was obviously already regretting saying anything at all and turned her back to them. A moment later she was inside. And Barbie and Victor were high-fiving each other. Now they had something. It wasn't much, but they could build a segment, a story around that one comment.

"Smart move coming here when we did," Victor said with admiration.

"Thanks. You ready to head back into the studio and put this together?" They had plenty of time to put something compelling together and it would likely be their lead story. Her lead story. Barbie beamed all the way back to the studio.

35

Lauren hurried inside and bolted the door securely behind her. Stupid, so stupid of her to let that reporter bait her. She hadn't said much, but she knew they would create something damaging with it. One simple comment would come back to haunt her. She shrugged off her wet winter coat and shook off her boots. It felt cold in the condo. She always pushed the heat down a few notches in the morning when she left. She pushed the heat back up, flipped on the fireplace and collapsed on the sofa, pulling a soft throw around her. What was she going to do with herself? She felt like she'd lost everything, her job, her reputation, and possibly her freedom, if people believed she'd actually killed someone.

Maybe she should get away, go out of town for a few days, maybe even back to Seattle to visit friends. Then she realized that wasn't possible. One of the conditions of bail was that she stayed local, no out of town travel. And the wedding was this coming Saturday.

As much as she'd been looking forward to it, now she was dreading it. How could they still have it? If they postponed or cancelled, they'd lose everything—it was much too late for that. All the food and flowers had been ordered. This was a disaster. Would people even still come if they did have the wedding? Would David want to still marry her? Especially now? Lauren felt the tears coming again and burrowed down in her blanket, feeling very sorry for herself. She couldn't imagine how she was going to get out of this mess.

36

David felt the strange vibe in the office the minute he walked in. People said hello, but there were averted glances and awkward hesitations. It immediately put him in a foul mood and after he found an over-sized mug, he filled it with black coffee and went into his office to hibernate, closing his door tightly behind him. He never closed his door unless he was in a meeting, but this morning he wanted to try to block everything out so he could focus on work and get his mind off the whirlwind of insanity around him.

Not five minutes later, his phone buzzed and it was Helen at the front desk announcing that Randy, his 'favorite client' as he referred to himself, was on the line. David gritted his teeth. "Thanks; please put him through."

"David, how are you?" Randy's booming voice was so loud David had to hold the phone away from his ear.

"What's going on Randy?" He asked, ignoring the question of how he was.

"You free at lunch today? I have something I want to run by you." David checked his calendar. He was free and though he'd ordinarily be tempted to say he couldn't make it, today he actually welcomed the invitation. Even though it was Randy, it would still help to get his mind off everything. He knew that a meeting with Randy meant talking about Randy the entire time, and today that might be okay. They agreed to meet at the Club at noon. A few minutes later, there was a knock on the door.

"Come on in."

Billy entered the office and shut the door behind him. He didn't sit, just paced around the room as he talked.

"How're you holding up?"

"Hanging in there." Like Lauren, he'd barely slept and guessed that it wasn't too hard to tell from the shadows under his eyes.

"You look like hell." Billy confirmed. "How's Lauren doing?"

"The same. They sent her home as soon as she got in this morning. Leave of absence. Kind of figured they'd have to do that."

"Yep. No choice really, 'til this all blows over." He looked at David thoughtfully. "This will blow over right? No chance there's anything to it?"

"No way. I absolutely trust Lauren and I know her."

"Good. So what about the wedding? Is it still on? Probably going to postpone I imagine?"

"It's definitely still on. I don't know about postponing. We need to talk about that tonight I guess."

"Well, let me know if I can do anything. You know you have our complete support—both Chuck's and mine. We talked about it earlier."

"Thanks, I appreciate that. Is Chuck in today? I didn't see his car outside?"

"He and Katy are seeing a marriage counselor this morning. Nothing major—just a few bumps in the road." Billy left and David tried to dive into his work, but it was hard to focus. He started wondering if they should postpone the wedding until this craziness died down. He didn't want to, but if they married now, it wouldn't exactly be the wedding of Lauren's dreams. More like a circus. Yet he didn't want to put it off.

Several hours later at lunch, Randy asked him the same question.

"It's up to Lauren, whatever she wants to do."

Randy dipped the end of his rare roast beef sandwich into a small dish of au jus and took a bite. As soon as he swallowed he said, "You know, if you go through with the wedding, it'll be like you're thumbing your nose at all the naysayers, and showing total support and trust in Lauren."

"I agree and plan to share that with Lauren. Ultimately, it's her call though. I wouldn't blame her if she wants to postpone. It's a difficult time, not exactly a time of celebration."

"Attitude is everything. They close on any other leads? It seems like they've been working hard on this. They even came around questioning me, can you imagine?" That got David's attention.

"Why would they question you?"

"Eric did a little work for me on the side, parking cars. We had a disagreement. He and his buddy took one of my Lamborghini's for a joyride and hit some rocks that damaged the paint. You can guess I wasn't too happy about that."

"What did you do?"

"We had an arrangement; they'd work doing odd jobs for me until the damage was paid off. We disagreed on the length of the term. They just decided one day that they were done, and I felt they hadn't worked enough."

"So what did you do?" David asked again.

"Nothing. Just yelled and screamed and that was the end of it. Plus I had an alibi for the time period they thought Eric was killed."

"Oh?"

"Yeah, wife and I were in all night. She'd made a great dinner, her meatballs and sauce rock, and I went to bed early that night. Food coma did me in." He flashed a grin before diving into his French dip for another bite.

David still had half of his burger left, but he'd suddenly lost his appetite. His mind swirled with what Randy had just divulged. Memories came rushing back of Randy in college, and the multiple occasions where his temper had gotten him into trouble. He'd been even more of a hothead then, blew up easily and when he did, nothing around him was safe. He liked to smash things when he was mad, anything he could get his hands on, a baseball bat was a particular favorite.

He once used a baseball bat to thoroughly demolish a vehicle parked outside the frat house, annihilated the windshield with one blow and left nasty dents all over. David and several others had watched him do it with a mixture of awe and disgust. They hollered at him to stop, but he ignored them until he was done and his anger was somewhat sated. The boy whose car he destroyed did nothing about it. He didn't dare. He'd made the mistake of dating Randy's recent ex-girlfriend.

David hadn't thought much about Randy's legendary temper. He hadn't seen any signs of it since he'd moved to Waverly. College was a long time ago, and people grew up. But maybe they didn't change that much. After all, he was still a self-centered loudmouth, why wouldn't he still have the temper too? He'd have to ask Jake about Randy.

"So, the reason I wanted to talk to you," Randy began, and David snapped his attention back.

"I have a chunk of money in an account offshore. I'd like to invest it. Do I need to move it here first?"

"How much money are you talking?" David was intrigued. He wouldn't have pegged Randy as sophisticated enough to have an offshore account.

"About five million." David raised his eyebrows. Where did Randy get that kind of money?

"That's a very large chunk."

"I've made some good investments, now I want you to make a few more for me."

On his way home from work, David called Jake and told him about his conversation with Randy.

"So, is he a suspect?"

Jake hesitated for a moment before answering. "No. he's not an official suspect. Listen, I don't like the guy any more than you do, but he doesn't really have a motive. He just has a bit of a temper. I don't see him killing the kid over the argument they had. There's no evidence to support the idea, and he has an alibi. He was home with his wife all night."

"Wives don't make the strongest alibis."

"I agree. But still, the fact remains that there's not a scrap of evidence to tie Randy to the murder. His prints aren't on the golf club." He didn't add that Lauren's were, but it's what they were both thinking.

"Okay. It would just be almost satisfying if he was the guy, you know?" David was drained; it had been a long day.

"I know. We're still working on this," Jake reassured him. "Some of us are not convinced that Lauren did this."

"Thank you. It's good to hear that." David hung up, pulled onto Lauren's street and was dismayed to see the media vans lining the street. There were at least a half dozen of them. When they realized who he was, they flew out of the vans and came running, calling out his name. He refused to even look their way. David walked in the door and once again, the condo smelled amazing. Lauren had been cooking up a storm. He set his briefcase down, took off his coat and shoes and then walked into the kitchen and gave Lauren a kiss hello.

"How was your day?" he asked and looked at the pots bubbling away on the stove. One held boiling water and the other was a huge stockpot full of spicy tomato sauce and oversized meatballs. Lauren opened a box of rigatoni pasta, dumped it into the water and added a pinch of salt.

"Surreal. It's better though, now that you're home."

"Have those vultures been out there all day?"

"Since about three this afternoon. Once they realized I wasn't still at school they caravanned over here. Except for one reporter who was sharp enough to realize I wouldn't be staying long today."

"Oh yeah? Which one was that?"

"Barbie Montgomery. She's blonde and looks like she's twelve."

"You didn't talk to her, did you?" David hoped not.

"Yeah, but just a brief comment, one sentence. I don't think it'll be too bad." She bit her lower lip again. She'd been biting it all afternoon, worrying about how Barbie would showcase her statement.

"You know what Evan said, you have to just say 'no comment', even if they provoke you."

"I know. She got me at a weak moment. It won't happen again." She turned to the cupboard and got out two pasta bowls. Once the pasta drained, she filled the bowls and then added sauce and meatballs. "I hope you're hungry," she said as she handed David his dinner and they sat down to eat.

David's stomach grumbled in response and he remembered he'd only eaten half his lunch. "I'm starving."

They dug in as David told her about his lunch with Randy and when she started to look excited, he felt bad squashing her hopes by telling her what Jake had said and that he was not a suspect.

"That's too bad. I was hoping they might be getting close on someone else."

"Jake said they're still working hard on it, and that he and a few others aren't convinced that you did anything. There's still the other prints on the club. That should be enough to prove reasonable doubt, hopefully, and if they can figure out who those prints belong to they'll be closer to knowing who really did this."

"We close on the house tomorrow. Is there any danger that won't happen now because of this?" Lauren felt like her whole world was crumbling around her.

"It shouldn't. I think we would have been contacted by now if there was going to be a problem. As long as we show up with a big check, we should be okay." He smiled then, trying to lighten the mood and Lauren smiled back. She knew this must be incredibly hard on him as well.

"How was everyone in the office?" she asked.

"Fine. Billy assured me that he and Chuck give us their complete support." Lauren didn't need to know about the averted glances and awkward hesitations. He'd deal with it.

"Good, I'd hate for this to make things difficult for you at work."

"We should talk about the wedding though," David began. "Do we still want to go forward this weekend? Or do you think we should postpone? It's fine with me either way, but I feel badly that you won't get your dream wedding. That the vultures outside will ruin it."

"And that people might not come," she added. "I know. I've been thinking about this all day too, going back and forth on what's best. What do you think?" She knew what she wanted to do, but didn't want to push him into anything he wasn't sure of.

"I'd like to still do it this weekend. I don't want to wait, unless you do." Lauren felt her first real moment of happiness in an otherwise horrible day.

"I definitely want to go through with it. I can't wait to marry you."

"We'll likely take a lot of criticism for not postponing, but I think it will show them how much I trust and support you as well."

37

David met his grandfather the next evening, Tuesday, at the pub for their weekly dinner. The media was still camped outside the condo and David felt terrible for Lauren. She dreaded facing them so much that she was avoiding leaving the house unless it was absolutely necessary. When she did, several vans followed her wherever she went and called out to her the minute she got out of her car. They didn't do that with him. He'd never given them satisfaction of a second glance, let alone a comment they could use, so they didn't bother to follow him, just sat there waiting patiently for Lauren. Hoping she'd crack and give them something they could use.

"It's pretty bad," he admitted to his grandfather after they'd put their dinner order in and were relaxing with their drinks and a bowl of peanuts.

"What's Jake have to say? He got any other leads they're close on? Or are they putting all their energy on Lauren?"

"I'm not sure. Jake doesn't say much. He has to be careful, considering my relationship to Lauren."

"He could tell you if they've got anyone else they're seriously looking at though."

"He said they're still working hard on it, exploring every lead. That's all I know." David sighed and reached for another peanut.

"They set a date for trial yet?"

"No, she goes back to court in two weeks and they'll set a date then I guess." They changed the subject for a bit and Gramps filled him in on all his neighborhood gossip. Their pizzas came right out and they dove in. The pub was starting to fill up as people streamed in after work.

"That guy looks familiar," his grandfather said as a tall, sandy-haired guy wearing a blue blazer walked through the door and headed for the bar. His back was to David so he didn't recognize him at first, but then he turned, and when he saw David, gave a wave and walked over to their table.

"Chuck, this is my grandfather. Gramps, Chuck is one of the partners at the firm."

"Great to meet you, finally. David's mentioned you often over the years."

"You, too," Gramps said as he reached for a slice of pizza.

"Well, I just wanted to say hello, I won't keep you from your dinner."

"You're welcome to join us," Gramps offered.

"Thank you. I'm meeting a buddy here at the bar though, so I'm off to try and find a seat."

He left and David and his grandfather resumed eating their pizza, which as usual was delicious.

"So, you said you thought Chuck looked familiar? Did you think he was someone else?"

Gramps thought about that for a moment.

"No, I don't think so. It's just that I'd seen him somewhere recently. I recognized his baseball cap, the dark green with the blue emblem. It's from that golf club you and Lauren play at, right?"

"Sure, I have the same one."

"He has a matching jacket too, one of those windbreaker things, same color green."

"Oh?" David grabbed a slice of the house special pizza, the Fenway, which had sausages, green peppers and onions. His grandfather ordered his usual, with sliced tomato, basil and fresh mozzarella.

"Yeah, and I just remembered where I'd seen him. Last time Al and I were down at the lake, he was there, fishing. Al says he's seen him there a few other times."

"No kidding, I never knew he liked to fish."

"You'd be surprised what you don't know about people you think you know well." He grinned as he slid a fourth piece of pizza onto his plate. "I really shouldn't. Mouth says yes and stomach says no. Mouth wins, as usual."

David reached for a fourth slice himself. This was also part of their routine. His grandfather always protested that he shouldn't eat so much, but couldn't help himself. His grandfather's comment made him wonder if he had any doubts about Lauren.

"You know Lauren couldn't possibly have done this, right?"

His grandfather looked up at him, his eyes serious now.

"Are you asking me if I think she did this? Or if it's possible? Two different things. It's most certainly possible. It was her club; if she was really angry she could have whacked him good and then shoved his body into the lake. But do I think she did it? No, of course not. Why, are you having doubts?"

"No!"

"Good, because you're marrying her in what—three days now? Any doubt at all would be a hellava thing to have hanging over the marriage."

"No doubt. I trust Lauren completely."

"Good. Getting married now, instead of postponing is the right thing to do, and smart. You'll be sending that message publicly, and seems to me that girl needs all the support she can get."

38

Jake had never felt so torn up about a case before. He'd been excited when the idea of Randy as a suspect was raised, as it would have made sense for the killer to be someone like that; unlikeable and hot-tempered. The idea of Lauren as Eric Armstrong's killer had never made sense to him, not for a moment. Yet the evidence was compelling. And there was motive and there were rumors, and usually where there was smoke there was fire. Usually.

Fortunately, the fact that there were other prints on the club in addition to hers could be enough reasonable doubt. He hoped so. Actually, what he really hoped for was a lead that would point him to the real killer and then Lauren would never have to worry about 'reasonable doubt.'

He kept going over everything, all the details in the case. There had to be something they were overlooking. He had a request in to the judge to get permission to require fingerprint testing from all country club members and staff. Since the golf club had been taken from inside the country club, there was a strong likelihood that whoever removed it and used it as a weapon either worked there or was a member.

There wasn't a guarantee that he'd be granted permission though. It could be viewed as an invasion of privacy. Jake was hoping the judge would see the necessity. He had a reputation for being reasonable.

He spent the next hour and a half combing through the stack of paperwork pertaining to the case. Most of it he'd seen before, transcripts from all interviews with the family and Eric's friends, autopsy results that pointed to time and cause of death, and stuck inside the autopsy folder was a copy of Eric's birth and baptismal certificates.

The baptismal certificate was still in its envelope and the date was just a few days ago. It must have recently arrived and been added to the folder. Jake slipped it out of the envelope, intending to give it a cursory glance and then put it right back, but then a name on the certificate jumped out at him. Chuck was Eric Armstrong's godfather. Funny that it hadn't been mentioned before. He wondered what the relationship was to the family...if Chuck was a relative, cousin or something? Not that it was likely important, but it was a detail he could follow up on. He placed a call to the Armstrong house and Judith answered.

"Hi, Mrs. Armstrong, Jake here. Quick question for you. I'm going over some paperwork here at the office and noticed that Chuck is listed on Eric's baptismal certificate. I'm just trying to establish Chuck's relationship to the family; is he a relative? Friend?"

"Please, call me Judy. Chuck's not a relative. He was

once a very good friend. He and my husband had a falling out years ago and drifted apart. He still stayed close to Eric though, always made a point to see him and remembered his birthday and on Christmas. He's a good person, just marches to a different drummer." She gave a nervous laugh.

"What do you mean by that?" He didn't know Chuck at all, even though David had worked with him for years. It was always Billy he talked about and did things with outside of the office. All Jake knew about Chuck was that he'd been married for about a year and was supposedly very good at his job. He wasn't the most personable broker, but his clients were happy with the results he achieved for them.

"Nothing, it's just a saying. He's always been a bit of a loner I guess, kind of moody. The fight that they had was so stupid that I don't even remember what it was about. But they haven't spoken since. They're both so stubborn."

"Is Ted around? I'd love to circle back with him, make sure we're not missing anything here."

"You don't think Chuck had anything to do with this, do you? He loves Eric, he'd never hurt him," Judy said.

"I'm not thinking anything like that. Just doing my job, trying to make sure we have all the information possible in case something turns up that might lead us in the right direction."

"But, I thought you already arrested someone for this? That teacher of his? The papers make it seem like it's an open and shut case with the murder weapon and finger prints. Though I find it hard to believe myself. She seemed like such a nice young woman. None of this makes any sense." Her voice broke a little and Jake felt for her.

"I agree with you on that. I'd like to come out and visit with Ted around 6:00 tonight if you think he'll be back by then?"

"He's usually home by 5:30, so that should be fine."

Jake hung up the phone and turned back to his desk. For the rest of the afternoon he intended to learn all he could about Chuck.

As far back as middle school, he'd known Chuck, or known of him. Chuck's family had moved to the area when Jake was in the seventh grade, and Waverly being a small town, he met everyone but tended to stay on the sidelines, happy to bask in Billy's shadow. Billy was the life of the party even then and kids always gravitated to him. While Billy had many friends, Chuck had very few.

He mostly kept to himself and was quiet. Jake recalled him sitting in the corner reading rather than joking with all the other kids. Normally someone like that would have been a total outcast, picked on and left out. But, Billy wouldn't allow it. He insisted on pulling Chuck out of his shell and including him in everything. Plus, even then, Chuck was a big kid, close to six feet tall and closing in on two hundred pounds. No one was going to mess with him.

Chuck was always around, but Jake couldn't recall ever having more than a one or two sentence conversation with him. He was there the night of the incident too, when Jake, Billy and Lauren were interrogated. Chuck had left at some point before the police arrived, so like the rest of the kids, he wasn't questioned with the same intensity that the three of them had been. Some details from that night were crystal sharp still in Jake's memory but the rest were hazy. He remembered seeing Chuck that night, but wasn't sure when he saw him last and exactly how early he'd left.

He knew that Chuck was an excellent student, especially in Math and Science where he took honors courses and still got top grades. He went to MIT, and majored in math. He knew from comments that Billy and David made over the years, that when Chuck graduated, he was looking at getting his PhD, until a phone call from Billy changed his mind.

Billy's uncle had gotten him into the training program at Warren Brothers, a top investment firm in Boston. Billy floated Chuck's resume to the recruiting manager and they didn't hesitate to invite him in. They loved to hire out of the best schools, especially Harvard and MIT. Billy was persuasive and the starting salary was attractive as well, so Chuck agreed to delay graduate school for a year or two. Once he discovered the mathematical challenges of the stock market and had some success, graduate school became an afterthought.

A few years in, once they'd established themselves and had a good client base, Billy once again persuaded Chuck to join him in a new venture. He wanted to open their own investment firm in their hometown of Waverly. Billy figured that a good majority of their clients would go with them and they'd make up for the ones that didn't by getting referrals from people they knew in Waverly.

Jake also knew from David that business was very good for their new company, which was now nearly fifteen years old. Billy was a natural salesman and handled the rainmaking and client schmoozing while Chuck stayed in the background, doing what he did best—playing with numbers. The firm grew steadily over the years to its current size of twenty employees and three partners.

Jake considered what he knew about Eric's father, Ted. He was a few years older than Chuck and he didn't recall them being friends during their school years. Ted had been born and brought up in Waverly but didn't attend the local public schools. He went to a private Catholic school in the next town and then like Chuck also attended MIT. Jake figured that was where they had likely struck up a friendship.

At a quarter to six, Jake shut down his computer and grabbed a small notebook to take with him. He arrived at the Armstrong house fifteen minutes later and Judy heard his car coming down the driveway, had the front door open and was waiting for him just inside.

"Come in. Ted will be right along." Judy led him to the kitchen table and returned a moment later with Ted behind her. He was dressed in a suit and tie and looked uncomfortable. He shook Jake's hand, then took off his jacket and loosened his tie before sitting at the table with them.

"Had to meet with clients today. Only time I ever put on that monkey suit," he said and Jake smiled in response.

"So, I was going through the case file paperwork and noticed that Chuck is Eric's godfather and was wondering what the relationship is? Judy explained that you used to be close friends."

Ted's eyes clouded over and a deep frown line appeared between his eyebrows.

"Used to be best friends. That was a long time ago though. We haven't spoken in well over ten years."

"Chuck stayed close to Eric, though?"

"He did. Never missed a birthday or Christmas gift. He was a lousy friend but a good godfather."

"Did he spend time with Eric too?"

"He saw Eric a few times a year. They'd mostly go fishing together and catch up on things."

"Do you know when he saw him last?"

"At least a month or so before he was killed. They went fishing on his birthday weekend."

"Anything unusual happen? Did Eric come home upset?"

"No. I don't think Eric was ever upset with Chuck. They always got along great. Chuck's a pretty mellow guy for the most part."

"What did you and Chuck fight about that ended your friendship?" Jake felt nosy asking the question, but depending on the reason, it could be relevant.

"You know, in retrospect, it was kind of stupid. But we were both stubborn and both felt we were right. It had to do with my wife, Judy. I felt that she and Chuck were getting too close, and were ganging up on me about different issues. Judy and I were going through a rough patch then and I admit I was jealous. Chuck criticized my relationship with Judy; said I didn't listen enough and a few other things. I didn't want to hear any of it. All I heard was my friend showing a little too much interest in my wife."

"Judy, do you still talk to Chuck?" Jake was curious to hear the answer to this question.

"Me? No. Of course not." She seemed surprised and a bit nervous by the question and Jake wasn't sure he believed her.

"Okay. Anything else I should know?"

"No, that's about it I think." Ted put his arm around Judy

and she snuggled close. They'd apparently resolved their differences.

"Thank you. I'll be in touch if we need anything else."

As Jake drove away, he couldn't help but wonder if there were still unresolved issues between Chuck, Ted and Judy.

39

The night before the wedding, after the rehearsal dinner at one of their favorite restaurants, David went over to Lauren's condo for a short visit before heading home for the night. As strange as circumstances were, they both wanted to follow tradition and not see each other right before the wedding. David was having some serious second thoughts though. It felt like such a black cloud hung over them.

"I don't know if we are doing the right thing, going through with this. Maybe we should postpone, hold off until the dust clears."

Lauren looked up at him in dismay. "Are you serious? You don't want to marry me tomorrow?" Her eyes welled up in an instant and David felt like a heel.

"Of course I want to marry you. It's just, well, the timing really couldn't be any worse."

"Well, if you don't want to marry me, I certainly don't want to talk you into doing something you don't want to do."

David stood up, walked to the window and said nothing for a few minutes. Then he walked back to Lauren and pulled her into his arms.

"I love you, you know that. You have to know that. I have no doubts about marrying you. I only questioned the timing." He smiled then and thought of his grandfather.

"What is it?" Lauren asked.

"I was just thinking about Gramps."

"What does he think about us getting married now?" Lauren looked nervous to hear the answer.

"He thinks we should do it and be proud of it. He doesn't believe in doing things half-way."

"I've always loved your grandfather." Lauren looked relieved.

The wedding went off without a hitch. Well, except for the parade of media vans lined up outside the reception hall. But, Lauren and David had instructed their guests to simply ignore them and to please not even stop for a 'no comment.' Even though there was a somber air that permeated the room at first, their family and friends shook it off and rallied around them to celebrate and support their union.

Lauren's dress fit like a dream and even the weather cooperated with a light and pretty dusting of snow, just enough to create a romantic mood. They were married at St. David's

Episcopal Church where Lauren was a parishioner and then the reception was at the Brentley Hotel, just outside Waverly's town line.

The evening flew by and before she knew it, Lauren and David were alone together in the honeymoon suite.

"Mrs. Bishop, I can't wait to spend the rest of my life with you." David made a show of carrying her over the threshold and then they were in the suite and kissing like they'd been apart for too long.

Lauren woke the next morning and felt a great sense of peace and contentment. She and David were officially husband and wife. She glanced over at him and felt a sense of wonder that this man was in love with her. She stretched and enjoyed the richness of the luxurious high thread-count sheets, which were satiny smooth and soft. They had all day to relax and enjoy themselves before heading home tonight.

The one thing they had agreed to postpone was the honeymoon. Since Lauren was supposed to stay local, they didn't want to push their luck by jetting off to the Caribbean, which is where they were originally scheduled to go. She didn't exactly know which island though because David wanted to surprise her. He said it had been a simple matter to postpone the trip.

When they arrived home the next night, there were several media vans waiting. Lauren was finding that the sight of them bothered her less and less. She'd developed the ability to finally put her blinders on and ignore them, no matter what they said.

"Lauren, were you thinking of Eric at all during your

wedding? Do you regret killing him?" This came from a petite red-haired reporter that Lauren didn't recall seeing before.

"Lauren, is your marriage a cover? A ploy to make you look trustworthy?" Lauren recognized the voice before she saw the fluffy blond hair of Barbie Montgomery. She opened her mouth automatically to tell her where to go, but David grabbed her arm and shot her a look that warned her to be quiet, to not let Barbie get to her. Thankfully, she bit her tongue and ducked inside as soon as David had the door open. Just when she'd thought she had such strong control, it was disconcerting to see how easily she'd almost lost it.

"She is evil," Lauren said as they put down their bags and took off their coats.

"She's just doing her job. Not that I could imagine having her job"

"I don't know how those people sleep at night."

"Come here." David pulled her towards him and kissed her thoroughly. When they broke apart he added, "Don't waste another moment of energy stressing about those goons. Let's go upstairs."

40

I've been tailing them," David's grandfather said proudly. The Tuesday after the wedding, David and his grandfather were having their usual pizza dinner at the pub. David hadn't seen his grandfather this energized and excited in a long time.

"You've been tailing Randy AND Chuck?" David was amused and intrigued. "For how long? Did you see anything interesting?"

"For the past few days. They're the last two people Jake's been asking about so I thought I'd see what's what."

"I didn't know Jake was even talking to Chuck."

"I don't think he has yet. He was out at the Armstrong's place asking them about Chuck. He was Eric's godfather you know."

"I didn't know that. How did you find out?"

"I still have friends inside. They keep me posted on the

interesting cases. Chuck is out of town until tomorrow. I imagine Jake will want to talk to him first thing."

David was impressed. Chuck was indeed away for a few days. He'd been out since last Wednesday, actually. His great Aunt had died unexpectedly and Chuck was the administrator for her estate. He flew back for the wedding, but had to return the next day to handle all the funeral arrangements.

Something just occurred to David. "So, if Chuck has been out of town, how have you been able to tail him?"

"Well, I followed him to the airport of course, to see if he really was going back to his Aunt's place. Looked like he was. He got on a flight to Minnesota again and I confirmed that's where she lives."

"So, you mostly followed Randy? Did you see anything interesting?"

"Sort of. Doesn't interest me much. I find this kind of thing disgusting, as you well know, but your friend Randy apparently has a lady on the side."

"Randy is not a friend, he's a client," David corrected and the fact that he had a mistress was not surprising.

"Whatever, he's a cheat. That's about all I saw though. He travels a lot too. Flew out to Vegas and Chicago this week, and to Dallas and Atlanta last week."

"Are you sure you want to be doing this? If Jake thought it was important to follow these guys he'd have someone doing it."

"Jake doesn't have the resources to have them followed, or enough of a reason to demand it if he did. This gives me something to do. I used to be quite good at this kind of thing you know." He reached for another slice of pizza and David did the same.

"I know you're good at it. I just wish they were closer on someone, so Lauren could get her life back."

Well, I'm on it. Chuck will be back tomorrow and we'll see what he's up to."

"I wouldn't waste too much energy there. Chuck's a decent guy. There's no way he's involved in this."

"You never know what people are involved with 'til you poke around and find out. What are you doing tomorrow night? You want to ride along?"

"While you tail my client and partner? I don't know about that."

"Oh come on, it'll be fun. We'll make a big thermos of hot chocolate and Peppermint Schnapps."

"Drinking and driving and tailing? Doesn't sound very law abiding to me." David grinned at his grandfather. He knew he wasn't a drinker and that there'd only be a splash of schnapps, just enough to add the minty flavor. It was fun to tease him, though.

"Right. So, I'll pick you up at 5:30 then." And before David could protest, he added, "After all, what else do you have to do?"

41

We've decided to hold off on adding new members right now. We'll be in touch in the spring once things open up again. We hope you understand. Happy holidays!" The e-mail message was from Chuck's wife, Katy, on behalf of the Girl's Group, the one that Julie and Katy had been so eager to include her in—before she was arrested. She deleted the e-mail and sighed. She supposed she couldn't really blame them. It wouldn't look good to have their newest member accused of murder. Might dim their luster just a bit. She was disappointed though, as it had sounded like a fun group and she was eager to make more friends in town. Her only close friend was Amy and she called her to commiserate.

"They're a bunch of stuck up snobs anyway if you ask me. You're better off without them. Why don't you come with me tonight to the women's group at church? We're going to bake pies for the holiday sale next week to raise money." Amy went to the same Episcopal Church that Lauren attended, but she was more involved. Lauren had been thinking about doing more at Church, maybe this was the right time.

"Okay, I'm in. I'll meet you there at 6:00."

Lauren pulled into the church parking lot a few minutes before six and saw that Amy's car was already there. She walked into the parish hall and as soon as Amy spotted her, she waved her over to where she and several other women were just starting to peel apples.

"Mindy and Sue, you know my friend Lauren?" Amy introduced them.

"I think I've seen you at the services before. Welcome." Mindy said and Sue added, "Great to see you here. Pull up a chair and dive in. There should be another peeler around."

Lauren spotted one a few chairs down, grabbed it and settled in next to Amy to start peeling. As other women joined them, Amy introduced Lauren to each person and all were friendly and welcoming. There wasn't a single hesitation or awkward moment. The evening flew by and Lauren found herself thoroughly enjoying it.

She thought more than once about the difference between these women and those in the girl's group. She didn't know those women well, but she knew them more than the women in the church group. Many of these women recognized her face from attending services, but they didn't know her. Still, they didn't judge her the way the women in the group did. It was enough that she was here with them, and she appreciated their warmth and kindness.

Lauren felt tears threaten as a rush of emotion overwhelmed her and she realized how tense and stressed she'd been these past few weeks. There was really nothing worse than being accused of something you didn't do and feeling defenseless to prove it. She hoped that Jake was having some luck surfacing other suspects. She was due in Court in two days to set a trial date and the thought of that terrified her.

42

Jake had a meeting set with Chuck for 1:00 p.m. He was going to duck out of the office during lunch to meet Chuck for a cup of coffee at Lola's diner. Jake had suggested that, as he knew it would be awkward for him to come to Chuck and David's office or, with Waverly being such a small town, for him to come to the police station. People were bound to talk and there was nothing really to talk about—yet.

Jake arrived a little before one and settled into a booth with a view of the front door. He ordered a cup of black coffee while he waited and kept an eye out for Chuck. It was his habit to always sit facing the entrance, so he'd be fully aware of his surroundings and see everyone that entered the restaurant. Not that it was so important in sleepy Waverly, but it had been in Boston and was ingrained in him now. He couldn't relax if he sat with his back to a door.

At one o'clock on the dot, Chuck walked in and Jake waved him over to their table. They'd both already had lunch and since this wasn't exactly a social call, Jake got down to business as soon as Chuck's tea arrived.

"Appreciate you coming down here," he began, and Chuck nodded. "As I mentioned, it's nothing to be alarmed about, really just a formality. We're making sure all our i's are dotted and our t's are crossed. When I was going through the thick stack of paperwork on Eric Armstrong, I noticed that you were listed as the boy's godfather and I just wanted to follow up on that, find out more about your relationship to the family and to Eric. Your name hadn't been mentioned previously, and as you may know we don't have much to go on."

"I thought you had a murder weapon with finger prints belonging to Lauren Stanhope?" Chuck seemed surprised to discover that Jake was still investigating other leads.

"I'm not convinced that Lauren did this, and her prints aren't the only ones on the golf club. She lost that club and anyone could have picked it up, maybe even intentionally, to throw blame her way."

"That seems a little far-fetched." Jake noted with interest that Chuck's jaw clenched and he seemed uncomfortable. Though to be fair, most people did seem uncomfortable when they were being questioned by the police.

"You'd be amazed how unbelievable the truth often is." Jake said, then added "You were at Lauren's wedding, right? Do you think she's capable of something like this?"

Chuck shrugged. "David is my business partner. I don't know Lauren well at all. Like you said, you never know what people are capable of."

"Right, well let's get back to your connection to Eric then. How did you come to be his godfather?"

"Ted and I were tight in college. He was two years ahead of me at MIT and we were in a few of the same classes and worked on some outside projects together. We were both into algorithmic research. We spent hours together working on different computer formulas and programs. We became best friends and when Eric was born, he asked me to be his god-father. He didn't have any brothers."

"So what happened? You two had a falling out? Judy said you haven't spoken in years."

"Yeah, we had a disagreement over a computer program I wrote. We both worked on it, but Ted wanted to continue our research together in grad school and I joined Billy at the investment firm instead and kept refining the program on the side. I told Ted I wanted to continue my research on my own and see if I could apply it to the stock market. He was furious; said I was selling out. I disagreed, and like they said, we haven't spoken since. It's kind of stupid I know, but it is what it is."

"But you still stayed close to Eric? Saw him often?"

"Not as often as I would have liked. He was a great kid. He loved to fish like I did. That was our thing. I'd take him down to the lake and we'd hang out for an afternoon. We never caught much, but we enjoyed our time together, catching up."

"When did you last see Eric?"

"It was right around his birthday. Maybe three weeks before he disappeared."

"What was his mood then, was he upset about anything?"

"He was quieter than usual, seemed a little down, kind of tense. I asked him what was going on and he said it was just the usual drama in the house. They fight a lot, Judy and Ted, and they'd go through stretches where it would get really bad and that would stress Eric out. He didn't like to be around them when they fought. Can't say that I blamed him."

"Did he mention having a girlfriend or a crush on anyone?"

"Not really. No one in particular. He said there were a few hot girls in his classes, but he wasn't dating any of them—not that I was aware of."

"Did he ever mention anything about Lauren, his teacher?"

"Yeah, he did, he liked her. He said she'd suggested meeting after class to talk about what was going on with him. He seemed flattered, said his friends thought she was hot too. He was a little confused about why she was being so nice to him."

"Really? Do you think he thought she was showing more than a normal teacher interest? That she was attracted to him or something?"

"I don't know. He was a good looking kid, big for his age and he said that he'd been hit on by older women before."

"Did he say Lauren hit on him?" Jake couldn't get a real read on what Chuck thought about this.

"No, I think he might have fantasized about it though. Lauren is a pretty girl. He wouldn't be normal if the thought hadn't crossed his mind."

"I suppose."

"I think Eric was just flattered that someone was showing him attention; that someone cared about him. He wasn't getting enough of that at home. His parents were too distracted being miserable with each other."

"Okay, did Eric mention anything else that was going on his life? Anyone or anything that might have been bothering him?"

"Well, there was one person he'd had a run-in with." Chuck told him pretty much verbatim what he'd already heard about Randy.

"Randy's a client of your firm. Do you think he could have had anything to do with this?"

"He's David's client. I've only met him in passing, played a game of golf with him once. He's not the most likable guy, but do I think he killed Eric? Damned if I know. I just hope if he did, you find him and put him away. Or whoever did this if it wasn't him. It just doesn't make sense to me. I miss him."

His voice broke and Jake sensed the emotion was genuine. Jake was feeling even more frustrated than before. Chuck not only had an alibi, he was at a dinner party with his wife and several others who could verify his whereabouts, but he also clearly loved the kid. He told Chuck he'd be in touch if they had any further questions and they both went their separate ways.

When he got back to the office there was an urgent message waiting for him from Dennis in the Boston DNA lab asking him to call ASAP. He tried him back and got his voicemail and then an email from his blackberry came through around 4:00 saying he was tied up at a crime scene and would call Jake on his cell as soon as he was finished. Jake tried not to get his hopes up, but Dennis sounded excited. Maybe… finally…they'd gotten a break.

43

David pulled into his grandfather's driveway a few minutes past 5:30 p.m. Gramps was filling a second thermos full of hot chocolate and added a few nips of peppermint schnapps to his foam cooler. He also had a bag of chocolate chip cookies.

"Ruth sent these over earlier today, made 'em just the way I like them, extra chocolate and no nuts. You ready to go?"

Gramps insisted on driving, so David hopped into the passenger side of his giant Cadillac, not exactly the most incognito car. He felt a bit foolish, but also a little excited to be going on a stakeout with his grandfather. It made him think of when he was a toddler, a young boy, and then a teen, and Gramps would let him ride around every now and then as he did his rounds. They'd never gone on a stakeout, though. This was a first.

"Randy's out of town, so we're on Chuck tonight. He usually leaves the office after you, right?"

"Right. He tends to come in later and stays 'til around six most nights." Gramps drove back toward the office and they parked a few blocks down, far enough away that they wouldn't be noticed and close enough that they could see who was coming out the front door. The area was quiet. It was dark and not much foot traffic, so Gramps didn't hesitate to crack open a thermos and pour a bit of peppermint schnapps into it. "Here you go," he handed the doctored thermos to David and then fixed his own. "Cheers!" He held his drink up and tapped it against David's.

"This is fun, huh? Cookie?" He held the bag out and David reached in, grabbed one and took a bite. They were still soft in the middle and delicious. A few cookies later and a little past six, Gramps spotted Chuck coming out the door.

"Time to rock and roll." He capped his hot chocolate, put it carefully into the tote bag and then started the motor. As soon as Chuck pulled out of his parking spot and started down the street, Gramps began to follow him, staying several cars back so he wouldn't be noticed. He fell back further once the traffic thinned out and they realized where Chuck was headed.

"He's going out to the Armstrong's. I thought they didn't speak," David said.

"Looks like he has something to say now." Gramps stopped a block away from the house, then once Chuck was inside, he pulled closer to see if they could get a glimpse inside. The house had large windows, was well lit and they could see three figures standing near the front hall window.

A moment later Judy walked away and it was just the two men.

The conversation looked intense, and Chuck was gesturing animatedly with his hands while Ted stood still, his hands in his pockets and his body tall and stiff. After about ten minutes, they shook hands and then Chuck came out, got into his car and drove off in a hurry.

They followed him to the pub, and through the oversized bay window, they watched him make his way to the bar and order a drink. For the next hour, they sat and sipped their hot chocolate and waited. Chuck ordered a second drink and a cheeseburger. He ate half the burger and downed the beer. Then his phone rang and he took the call and a minute later hung up, paid his bill and left.

As he left the building, they watched him pull out a pack of cigarettes and light one. He inhaled deeply and looked as if he was both loving and hating it at the same time. David couldn't remember the last time he'd seen Chuck smoke. He'd made a big deal out of quitting well over five years ago. He smoked half the cigarette then stubbed it out and tossed it in the trash. Ten minutes later, he pulled into his driveway and their stakeout was over.

"So, what do you make of that?" David asked.

"Not too hard to see he's damn upset about something. I'm thinking though, if it's a guilty conscience seems kind of strange to go visiting the victim's father, especially when he hasn't talked to the guy in years. Makes you wonder, what's up with that?"

44

The call back from Dennis with the DNA results finally came in a few minutes past five.

"Sorry I couldn't get back with you sooner. This day has been insane. So, the Armstrong case. We picked up something interesting. When Kelly was running the prints, she noticed a tiny spec of blood near the handle, and because of the location, got to wondering if it might be from the killer instead of the victim. The prints were Eric's, which makes sense, as he may have been the one who found the club, or grabbed it in self-defense. But,…the blood was similar to Eric's DNA but not identical, meaning it was someone related to him. Do you have DNA samples from his immediate family?"

"No, but I will get them, ASAP. Thanks Dennis, this could be the missing link we've been waiting for." Jake breathed a sigh of relief. It had to be Ted, Eric's father. It made sense, sort of. Ted was known to be short-tempered, and tensions had been high at home recently. Plus, it really was true that the majority of crimes were committed by someone who was close to the victim. They could get a rush on the DNA results and have this wrapped up within a few days, hopefully.

Two days later, the results came in. The first red flag that had gone up was when Jake had visited with Eric's parents and explained that they needed to take a DNA sample. There had been no hesitation or sign of nervousness whatsoever, not even from Ted. Jake was paying close attention, and in his experience over the years, he knew that people were not usually so cooperative unless they had nothing to fear.

That was the case here. Neither parent was a match for the tiny blood sample. Jake wasn't prone to fits of temper, but had a sudden urge to smash something out of sheer frustration. He needed to blow off some steam and to vent. A beer or two might do the trick. He called David who agreed to meet him in a half-hour at the pub.

There were plenty of seats at the bar when he arrived, and David was already there, about to take a sip of the draft beer that Patrick the bartender had just set down. Jake settled in the stool next to him and gratefully said *yes* when Patrick asked if he wanted one of the same.

"So, no progress, I take it?" David asked. Jake hesitated for a minute, then filled him in on the failed DNA tests. David looked as disappointed as Jake felt. He really had thought the DNA results would wrap things up so that Lauren would be exonerated and they could go on with their lives.

They talked about other things for a while, to get their minds off the case, and both ordered a second beer. Jake had just taken his first sip of the new beer when a new thought took hold. He'd been so frustrated by the bad DNA results and so sure that Ted was going to be the murderer, that he'd stopped looking beyond that conclusion. Now that he'd relaxed a bit, his mind wandered back and a missing piece fell into place. It was someone he'd considered earlier and discarded, but now it was a strong possibility.

"It has to be Chuck," he said out loud.

"Chuck? Where did that come from?" David set his beer down and looked confused.

"Just thinking back to a few conversations that don't add up. Judy mentioned that the reason Chuck and Ted ended their friendship was Ted's jealousy over Chuck growing too close to Judy. Chuck said it was because of a difference over a software program. What if there was something with Chuck and Judy, and what if Eric wasn't really Ted's son, but Chuck's?"

"What if he was?" David still wasn't following. "Even if he is his real father, it doesn't mean he's also the murderer."

"No, but it's more likely. Especially if it's his blood on the golf club."

"Well, that's simple enough then; we just get a DNA test from Chuck, right?"

Jake was silent for a moment.

"We still don't really have a motive yet, though. A spot of blood on a golf club might not be enough to get a conviction."

"So, what then?"

"I have an idea, and a possible motive; just a theory, but if

I'm right and we can get Chuck to confess, then the DNA will seal it. But, I need your help if you're up for it?"

"Of course, anything. What do you want me to do?"

45

The next day, David stayed later than usual. He left his office door open just far enough that he could see the main entrance and by a quarter past six, knew that he and Chuck were the only two people left in the building. He shut his door then, and placed a call to Jake.

"Are you ready?" Jake asked him.

"I think so. Are you sure this stuff is working?" Jake had given him a wire to wear under his shirt so that his conversation with Chuck would be recorded and also so Jake could hear it live. Jake and Toby, one of his officers were outside in a surveillance van, ready to come in at the first sign of trouble.

"You're good to go." David hung up and replayed what he and Jake had discussed about how the conversation should go. He took a deep breath, opened his door again and walked down the hall to Chuck's office. His door was closed and the office was eerily silent. But Chuck's light was still on, and David knew he was still there because he was a stickler about electricity and would never leave his light on unless he was working.

He knocked lightly on the door and after a long moment Chuck said to come in.

David walked in. Chuck had two computer screens lit up and was running a program on one while looking at about a dozen stock charts on the other.

"You're working late tonight," Chuck commented.

"Yeah, I've gotten behind on a few things, needed to catch up." He sat in one of two chairs opposite Chuck's desk.

"So, what's up?" Chuck never was one for idle chit chat.

"Well, you know the business with Lauren, the Eric Armstrong case."

"You'd think it was the only case the media has to focus on." Chuck laughed and David relaxed a bit. Chuck seemed to be in a good mood.

"Yeah, Lauren's been a little stressed, as you can imagine. How's Katy doing?" David thought asking after Chuck's wife might be a way to ease into the more difficult conversation.

"She's good, real good." Chuck actually smiled and David was caught off-guard a bit. "We haven't formally announced it yet, as it's not quite three months now, but she's pregnant." David knew they'd had a hard time getting pregnant and this would be their first child.

"That's great news. Congratulations."

"Thanks, so what's going on with you?"

"Well, I'm wondering if you might be able to shed some light on something. We're still trying to make sense of this whole thing and Lauren has been wracking her brain trying to remember anything that could help. Conversations she had with Eric, things that didn't seem important at the time, but that might be. We still don't have much to go on."

"Okay." Chuck waited for him to continue.

"Well, it's the strangest thing, and I don't know if it has any importance, but Lauren thought she remembered Eric saying something about finding out who his real father was, that he thought it was you." That was a lie, but Chuck wouldn't know it, and David hoped to throw him off-balance.

"That's ridiculous," Chuck said, but David noticed his hand was clenched so tightly around his pen that his knuckles were white.

"Is it?" David asked. He stood up and walked toward the window. He was too agitated to sit still as now he understood Chuck's motive, and he was furious to think that Chuck had used Lauren to throw suspicion off himself.

"You've always denied the affair with Judy, and now your wife is finally pregnant. Having Eric come forward would knock everything off-balance, and you like everything perfect, no messiness."

"That's ridiculous. You know me better than that." Chuck's voice was calm and measured but a flush was creeping across his face and David noticed a muscle twitch in his jaw. The key to breaking his resolve would be to make him mad enough that he'd snap. David had seen it happen before. Chuck was very tightly wound. He didn't like it when things didn't go his way. Everyone in the office knew to steer a clear path when he was in one of his moods. He could switch into a bad mood in an instant.

Another thought dawned on him then as he thought back

to his earlier conversations with Lauren and Jake. It was a bit of a reach, but it made sense, especially given the weapon that Chuck had used. Even if it wasn't true, it wasn't likely to go over well with Chuck. But would it be enough to push him over the edge? He hoped so. David leaned against Chuck's desk and looked him straight in the eye, "You killed Nancy too, didn't you? Lauren told me all about it. She was there as you well know."

Chuck said nothing at first. But then he stood up and faced David. His face was totally red now from rage and his eyes seemed distant and detached. He stayed silent for a moment longer and then he let loose, "Nancy was a little bitch. We were supposed to go on our first date the next day. It took me a week to get up the courage to ask her out and then at the beach, after a few drinks she tells me that wants to go out with Billy instead, that he was the one she really liked."

"So you killed her?" David couldn't hide his disgust.

Chuck barely glanced his way before continuing, "I barely remember reacting, it happened so fast. We were alone for a minute or so in one of the dunes. I had a golf club in my hand as we'd all been taking turns hitting balls. Next thing I knew, I swung at her and she went down. I panicked and hit her again, threw the club and then ran off, and left a short while later. No one ever connected me to it. Stupid cops."

"So what happened with Eric then? Do you remember that?" David asked carefully, and stepped closer to the door, prepared to make a run for it if he had to.

Chuck's eyes glazed over and then seemed to come into focus again. He spoke slowly with a sense of detachment, almost like someone relaying a bad dream. There had been no hint of regret in his voice when he talked about killing Nancy, but there was a fleeting hint of possible regret when he talked about Eric.

"It was more an accident than anything else. We were fishing, one of our usual trips. Eric was on edge, his parents had been fighting, and then he overheard his mother on the phone talking to his aunt. She said something like, 'thank god he takes after his real father', and then, 'he's seeing Chuck tomorrow, that should calm him down.' Eric put two and two together, and was upset. Said he was going to talk to his teacher Lauren about it, that she'd helped him work through stuff before. Obviously I couldn't let that happen."

"So, you killed your own son?" David couldn't hide his disgust.

"It just happened. We were arguing about it the whole way back to the car. I didn't want him to say anything to anyone, but he couldn't let it go. I saw the golf club in the back of his car and asked him about it. It was a three wood, a big club. He said it was Lauren's, that she'd left it at the club and he grabbed it to give to her at school the next day. It was an opportunity and I acted quickly. As soon as he turned away, I hit hard, so he went right down and was out immediately. I thought it was kinder that way." He paused then and David felt a chill run over him.

"I panicked then, dumped the body and took the club with me. That's why they didn't find it at first. But then I thought it over and brought it back a few days later and left it where I knew it would be found. It was unfortunate for Lauren, but it was perfect really as it could tie her to both murders while getting me off the hook completely." Chuck smiled then and took a step closer to David. "That was the plan anyway. Does anyone else know about this theory?" he asked calmly.

David swallowed and said, "No, just Lauren and me." It was a chilling realization, to think how little he actually knew Chuck, and they'd worked side by side for years.

"Well, I don't really have to worry about Lauren. I'm not quite sure what to do with you though. I've always liked you." Chuck's expression had shifted yet again from fury to confusion then to resolve, and David felt goose bumps.

He took another step toward the door as Chuck reached into a desk drawer and then pulled out a very large, sharp knife. He held it up just as David was about to make run for it.

"Stop right there." Jake walked into the room holding a gun aimed at Chuck with Scott right behind him.

"So, it's really all over then?" Lauren had her arms wrapped around David's neck and leaned in again to hug him tightly.

"It's over." David had called her on the way home, after watching Jake take Chuck away in handcuffs. He filled her in and then pulled her in for a kiss as soon as he'd walked in the door. They collapsed on the sofa and clicked on the TV and it was already all over the news. Relief swept over both of them.

"I still can't believe it was Chuck. That's just crazy," Lauren said.

"If you'd seen him, seen his face, then you'd understand. I

always thought he was a little off, but I didn't realize to what extent. He's just crazy enough to cross the line that most of us have all considered at one time. He actually went there, not once but twice. I called Billy on the way home too, and filled him in. He wasn't as surprised as I expected him to be. Said Chuck had been on meds for years. They had that in common too. But Chuck struggled with mental health issues that we never fully understood. He's brilliant, a mathematical genius, but he's missing a key empathy gene. Not a true sociopath but able to distance himself enough to do something like this, yet pull back and continue on to live a relatively normal life."

"I'm just glad it's over. Now we can enjoy being newly-weds."

"Well, funny you should mention that." David opened his briefcase and pulled out a colorful brochure with pictures of white sand and clear blue waters. "I've been holding on to these for a while. You know how you've always mentioned wanting to go to the Cayman Islands?" Lauren nodded. "Well, I paid for this trip months ago. I just need to call back and confirm the dates. How does the next school vacation sound to you? I'd say sooner, but you'll be heading back to work now."

"That sounds wonderful! And I can't wait to get back to work. School vacation is perfect." She leaned over and gave David a happy kiss. He pulled her in close. Now that Lauren had been cleared, he couldn't wait to start the rest of their lives together.

~The End~

AUTHOR'S NOTE

Dear Reader,

I hope you enjoyed the story. I welcome any feedback you may have, and would love to hear what you loved, liked, or even disliked, as well as what you might like to see next. Please drop me a note anytime at **pamelamkelley@gmail.com**

I also write sweet romances. SIX MONTHS IN MONTANA, is the first of my romance series set in Montana. If you'd like to take a look at that, please check out the excerpt and/or link below.

Coming soon is a new cozy mystery series that is a spin-off of TRUST. It's called MOTIVE, and features former law firm investigator Jane Cho. Jane has a special gift with numbers and computers, but after almost getting killed on the job, she turns in her notice and escapes to Waverly to open a comfort food shop. But when she meets Jake, the Waverly assistant sheriff; he tempts her to help him with an unusually challenging case.

I have a favor to ask of you. Please consider taking a moment to leave a quick review with your thoughts. Your review will help spread the word and help new readers find books they might enjoy. Here's the link, **http://amzn.to/1gFnSk7** Thank you so much!

~Pam

Here's the link for my email signup. I hate spam, and generally just send out new release alerts and updates on special offers, giveaways and early bird discounts. **http://eepurl.com/IZbOH**

ABOUT THE AUTHOR

Pamela Kelley lives and works in Plymouth, MA and has always been a huge book worm. She worked as a journalist many years ago and in recent years as a food writer for local papers. She is very excited to finally be following her passion to write the kinds of books she loves to read.

Other books by Pamela M. Kelley:

Check out my sweet western romance, SIX MONTHS IN MONTANA. It's a modern marriage of convenience story.

http://amzn.to/JmokZl

Excerpt and recipe on the following pages!

1

This is a joke right?" Christian Ford looked at his lawyer and best friend, Travis Jones, in disbelief. Now he understood why Travis had insisted that he come by his office for an official reading of his grandfather's will. "Are you seriously telling me that he changed his will less than a month before he died, and added this condition?"

"I'd love to tell you I'm kidding, but your grandfather was very clear about what he wanted." Travis added, "I tried to talk him out of it. Told him you haven't even seen her in years. But he was insistent, said he ran into her at the market last month. She was home for a quick visit, and they got to chatting."

"Doesn't she live in New York City now?" Christian hadn't seen, or thought of Molly in years.

"She does. Works for one of the large hotel chains. Sounds like she's done pretty well too."

"So this makes absolutely no sense then. Her life isn't here." Christian glanced around the office, not really seeing the varnished dark wood bookcases, or the view out of the window behind Travis, which overlooked Main Street in Beauville, Montana, a small town just outside Bozeman. Main Street served as the center of town, and most of its small shops and businesses were along this stretch.

"Your grandfather seemed to think she'd be better off here."

"It's absolutely ridiculous. She'll never agree to it. Why would she?"

Travis leaned back in his plush leather chair and picked up the will, shuffling the pages until he found the passage he was looking for.

"Well, you just have to stay married for six months. She'll be free to go after that if she wishes, and it might be worth her while."

"Have you called her yet?" Christian was having a hard time wrapping his head around this. His grandfather had always marched to his own drum and had had plenty of ideas about how Christian should do things, but he'd never meddled to this extreme before.

"I spoke with her briefly yesterday. She's on her way here, meeting us in an hour at Delancey's."

"We're not meeting here, in the office?" Delancey's was the best restaurant in the area.

"Given the situation, I thought the least we could do is buy her dinner."

2

Molly Bishop was tired and annoyed, though admittedly curious. It had already been a long day. She'd juggled her schedule a bit, going in to work earlier so she could duck out and catch a four o'clock flight. She made it, just barely, and it was an hour into the flight before she felt herself finally starting to relax. With the two-hour time difference between New York and Montana, she'd just about make it to dinner by seven. She'd also arranged for someone to fill in for her tomorrow and, truth be told, she could use this short break. Molly loved her job as assistant general manager at the Clarendon Hotel in Manhattan, but on a good day it was stressful, and lately there had been more fires than usual that had needed to be put out.

The hotel was an impressive one, but it was old and badly in need of renovating. In the past few months that had become painfully evident, as one major breakdown after another had needed attending to: the water heater had burst in the basement, creating a huge mess; two stoves in the kitchen had stopped working in the same week and, most damning of all, a famous reviewer had described the Clarendon online as 'old and drab, like a beautiful woman who is unfortunately showing her age'.

Molly thrived on the pace and excitement of running a top hotel in New York City. The energy there was like nowhere else. Things were always happening, and she was right in the middle of it, making sure that everyone who stayed at The Clarendon was well taken care of. That was noted in the same critical review: 'Though the hotel is desperately in need of a face lift, their standard of service remains as excellent as ever'.

Molly put a copy of the review in her scrapbook and had high hopes for her own career review next week. She was overdue for a promotion to general manager, the dream job she had been working toward for years, and it felt like it was finally about to happen. Obviously, it couldn't take place unless there was an opening for her to move into, but the current GM had been with the organization for seven years, a long time in the hotel world, and Molly hadn't been able to help but notice that Paul had recently been in several hush-hush meetings with the hotel's owners. Change was definitely in the air.

When the plane landed and Molly stepped outside, she immediately felt the sense of peace that always swept over her when she returned to Montana. As much as she loved New York, Montana still felt like home. The air here always had a calming effect on her. She tensed up a bit though, as she got into her rental car and started driving toward Beauville. Travis hadn't said much on the phone, just that there was something in Christian Ford's grandfather's will that concerned her, and that they should meet immediately to discuss it.

She couldn't imagine why Christian's grandfather had thought to include her in his will. When she'd run into him last month at the grocery store, it had been the first time she'd seen him in almost ten years. Once they'd got to talking though, the years had fallen away, and it seemed like only yesterday that she and Christian had been next door neighbors and best friends. They'd even shared a dog. Toby had been a stray that showed up one day and stayed, going back and forth between Molly's house and Christian's. When Molly was just fourteen, her father had died suddenly of a heart attack, and although Uncle Richard, her father's brother, lived in Beauville, her mother had had no other family in the area. They'd moved to New York two months later, to Brooklyn, where her Aunt Betty lived, and it had been decided that Toby would stay with Christian. Once a dog had enjoyed all that Montana could offer, how could he live in the city? It had made perfect sense at the time…But now Molly saw dogs everywhere she went in Manhattan.

Molly pulled into Delancey's parking lot at a few minutes before seven. It looked like they were doing a good business for a Wednesday night. Delancey's was one of only three restaurants in town and was without question the best. They were known for steak and Molly's stomach rumbled at the thought of it. She'd missed lunch and hadn't eaten on the plane, except for a small bag of pretzels.

She grabbed her purse and headed into the restaurant. Travis and Christian were already seated at a corner table and waved her over. She recognized Travis immediately, as she'd seen him briefly the last time she was in town. Both her mother and Aunt Betty were living here now. They'd come to visit one of her mother's friends a few years ago, and after just minutes in Montana, Aunt Betty had fallen in love and easily talked her mother into moving back to the area. Aunt Betty loved to entertain and half the town was at her most recent party, including Travis.

Both men stood when Molly reached the table, and Christian pulled out a chair for her. He held out his hand and said, "Thanks for coming." Molly shook both of their hands before settling into her seat. She was surprised that Christian seemed a little nervous. It had been many years since she'd seen him, and he'd grown into an impressive looking man. He smiled and she caught her breath. He still had the cutest dimples, and when he smiled the effect was devastating. Molly had heard that he'd done very well running his grandfather's business and, over the years, had expanded, so that now he had almost fifty men working for him. She must have imagined that he looked nervous.

"Christian, I am so sorry for your loss. Your grandfather was a special man."

"Thank you." They made small talk for a few minutes, as the waiter brought Molly a glass of Cabernet and then they put their orders in. The wine was excellent, rich and smooth, and she'd just taken another sip when Travis got down to business.

"I figured we might as well get this out of the way first, then we can relax and enjoy our steaks." It seemed as though he was trying to make light of something, which Molly found odd. She'd thought it was sweet that Mr. Ford had thought to include her in his will. It had been wonderful to bump into him last month; he'd been as feisty as ever, even though it had also been clear that he had slowed down quite a bit. Still, Molly never would have guessed that he'd been sick. He'd been ninety-four when he'd died, and had lived well right up until the end, when he'd gone to bed one night and never woken up. She was more than surprised she featured in his will, and imagined he'd left her a small token to remember him by, maybe one of his crystal animals. He'd had quite a collection and Molly had always admired them as a child.

"As I mentioned on the phone, Mr. Ford thought very highly of you." Travis paused for a moment, glancing at Christian, before turning his attention back to Molly and clearing his throat before continuing. His voice was a little shaky as he continued—Molly had never seen him so flustered. Travis was always so cool and collected. This wasn't like him at all.

"Yes, so as I was saying, Mr. Ford liked you, quite a bit actually. So much so that he thought it would be a very good idea for you to marry Christian."

Molly almost spat out her wine. "What?" By the look on Christian's face, he didn't look too happy about the idea either. "I don't understand."

"After Mr. Ford ran into you, he stopped by my office the next day and added a provision to his will, a condition under which Christian will only inherit the Ford ranch if the two of you get married immediately."

Molly was speechless. No wonder Travis was a little flustered. If he didn't look so uncomfortable, she'd wonder if he was joking, but it was obvious that he was quite serious.

"This is ridiculous. Why would he do this?"

Travis looked at Christian, who then explained, "My grandfather approved of almost everything I've done, except when it came to dating. I haven't really been serious about anyone in years, and he wasn't thrilled about the ones I have dated. He'd been after me for a long time to settle down. I told him that you can't rush these things, but truthfully I have no interest in getting married and he knew it."

"Okay, but why me? No offense, but why on earth would I agree to this? You both know I live and work in Manhattan. My life isn't here."

"He always liked you, and knew we used to get along."

"We were just kids." Molly protested.

7

Travis jumped in to further explain, "It's really not that bad. You just have to stay married for six months. If you both want out after that, there's no problem."

"Yes, but even if I were open to doing this, I couldn't. I have a job and an apartment clear across the country. Unless a long-distance marriage would be okay?" It was a lame attempt at humor on her part, a way to lighten the mood. The whole thing was too surreal.

"No, that wouldn't work." Travis pulled the will from a manila folder and flipped to the last page, where the terms of this arrangement were apparently detailed. "According to his instructions, you need to marry within the month, and live together as husband and wife for at least six months after that."

Read the rest here, *http://amzn.to/JmokZl*

RECIPE

<u>Braised Short Ribs</u>

4 pounds bone-in short ribs (or 2 pounds beef brisket)
1.5 cups red wine (I like to use a fruity zinfandel or any red you like)
1.5 cups beef broth
1 large onion, sliced thin
One cup mushrooms, chopped
1 clove garlic, chopped
1 tablespoon olive oil
½ cup tomato sauce (any favorite sauce is fine)
1 tablespoon Dijon mustard
¼ tablespoon rosemary
¼ tablespoon thyme

Pre-heat oven to 300 degrees. On the stovetop, in a large, heavy dutch oven (I use a 5 qt enamel coated cast iron soup pot, but have sometimes just used a big stainless pot too), heat the olive oil over medium heat. When the oil is hot, add the meat and brown it on both sides until you have a nice crust, about 5-8 minutes or so per side. Remove the meat and let it sit. Add the onion and garlic to the pan and stir, scraping up the browned bits on the bottom. After about 5 minutes, add your mushrooms, and let them cook a couple of minutes. Then add your tomato sauce, wine, broth, spices, and mustard. Stir well and then add your meat and any juices that have collected, back into the pan; cover and throw it in the oven for 3 hours. Stir and serve over mashed potatoes or noodles. I like to make it at night and let it sit in the refrigerator overnight. I then scrape off the hard fat the next day, reheat on the stove and it's delicious.

Enjoy!
~*Pam*

Made in the USA
Las Vegas, NV
19 August 2022

53619287R00163